BLEEDING EDGE

a collection of
cyberpunk short stories
from Ramsey Lundock

a BlackWyrm book
Louisville, Kentucky

BLEEDING EDGE

A BlackWyrm Book
BlackWyrm Publishing
10307 Chimney Ridge Ct, Louisville, KY 40299

Printed in the United States of America.

ISBN: 978-1-61318-104-1
LCCN: 2011905685
Cover photo by Rene Jansa
Edited by Dave Mattingly

First edition: February 2011

Table of Contents

This book is dedicated to BlackWyrm
for giving me a second chance.

Information Superhighway

"On ramp's blocked, take the exit ramp." Sanichiro's voice crackled over the police radio.

With out bothering to respond Rachael cranked the wheel, bouncing the car over the cement medium and rocketing up the exit ramp. At the top of the ramp she spun the car. It emerged from the spin in the center lane, but slid over to the left lane.

Frank released his death grip on the passenger side armrest. His ebony skin and hair already covered with sweat. "Careful, some of us have families."

"Some of us don't," Rachael answered, shifting into overdrive. Her curly red hair bounced like a sea of fire over crazed green eyes.

Ahead three cars drove side by side at the same crawling speed.

"I'll brake middle, accelerate left." Sanichiro's voice again.

Rachael moved up behind the left hand car, until there was less than a foot between the bumpers. With no warning other than Sanichiro's, brake lights flashed on their right. For only an instant, the terrified faces of the car's occupants were visible. Their trusted computerized car taken over by hackers, they had no way of knowing Officer Sanichiro Murayama was now in control.

Rachael dove into the middle lane, with only a radiator hose's diameter between hers and the cars on either side. As promised the left hand car was moving faster than before, but it was hard to notice as it shrank in the rearview mirror.

The traffic was becoming thinner. The Road Master program was routing bystander vehicles away from the manual chase route. Rachael maneuvered around half a dozen more cars.

"The blue sedan is going to sideswipe you as you pass." Sanichiro spoke with a nearly apologetic tone. "I couldn't stop the program, but I can keep the car from braking."

Rachael slowed down, and edged her hood up along the right of the sedan's trunk. The electric luxury car began to swerve

1

into their lane. Rachael hit the clutch and brake simultaneously and steered into the space just vacated by the powder blue car. An instant later, the brake had been released, the accelerator was on the floor and the clutch let out.

"How much farther to the mark?" Frank asked turning green.

"Half mile and closing," Sanichiro again.

Rachael's right hand dropped to the stick shift and her thumb hovered over a newly welded button connected to wires wrapped down around the stick shift.

"What's that for?"

"You should know, you filled out the paper work for it."

"Oh, a grenade launcher."

For the first time Rachael took her eyes off the road to look up and give Frank a confused glance.

"For the laughing gas grenades."

"Nitrous Oxide has other uses too," Rachael smiled and pressed the button.

"Like wha... aaaa!" What ever he was going to say was left behind as the car rocketed forward.

The cityscape on either side blurred as it raced past. The dirty gray getaway vehicle appeared ahead of them. It was easy to tell electric cars with their autodrive systems ripped out. It was slow and wobbled from lane to lane like a drunk was at the wheel. The true battle was in the computer grid, using innocent bystanders to block the police.

"When I pass him, blow this turkey's brains out."

"No! Our job is to arrest suspects, not litter the street with bodies. Slow down in front of him to force him stop."

"Yes sir," Rachael sneered and positioned herself to pass the suspect. Just before she pulled along side, the fleeing vehicle staggered into her lane.

"Dumb move." The accelerator was smashed against the floor. The leading car's trunk crumpled up like a soda can crushed to go in the recycle bin. The car lurched ahead, for an instant leaving the ground as it was pushed by the more massive, more powerful police chaser. It veered to the left and spun out of control.

"What are you doing? If you damage the engine..."

"On that windup toy? I'm more likely to hit a nail on the road." She hit the clutch and brake again. The tires squealed in protest but stopped the car. Without missing a beat, the car was in

2

reverse. "Remember we have a steel frame and no crumple zones. This body was resurrected from the time when cars were cars."

"And unsafe at any speed. Your actions were reckless."

"I wouldn't exactly say wreck-less." She stopped the car next to the getaway vehicle whose engine had been compacted to half size by the concrete guard rail. In one fluid motion Rachael took the car out of gear, push the parking brake in, and unbuckled her seatbelt. She popped open her door and leapt out, drawing her gun.

In the wrecked car, a large, half dazed man worked frantically with a joystick wired into the dashboard. Rachael reached though the broken window and pressed her cocked gun against his temple.

"You've been a bad boy, haven't you?" she giggled.

Frank came up behind her, his gun still holstered, "Sir, would you please step out of your vehicle. You are under arrest on suspicion of armed robbery, fleeing arrest, and bypassing automotive safety systems. You have the right to remain silent. Anything you say..."

Frank and Rachael were still on the scene as the tow truck operator winched the wreck onto the inclining bed of the truck. The suspect was loaded into the back of an electric squad car. All that remained was for Rachael's car to be loaded into its trailer and taken back to the station. Rachael had put the car in neutral, but she walked away when it came to hooking the winch to the dented front bumper. The car was black and white, but there was no siren; the engine was loud enough to warn people. Every edge was sloped back slightly to reduce drag. All the space under the hood was occupied by the engine, so much so that the center of the hood was cut away, making room for the chromed air-intake vents. The tires were regular size, so as not to reduce speed, but the frame was low to the ground for better handling.

Rachael leaned against the center guardrail and watched her car get drawn slowly into the black and white trailer.

"Rachael Kurman, your behavior today was dangerous, irresponsible, bordering on insubordination, and unbecoming of a police officer." Frank walked up to her.

"I apologize," she said in a far-off voice. "I'm pretty sure I have two more headlights, but could you order some more turn signals?"

"Are you listening?"

"Yes. That car and I are monsters you keep caged up until you want us to attack something. We are a disgrace that would be long buried if we didn't bring in the bad guys respectable people can't catch."

"Are you talking back to me?"

"Am I wrong?"

Frank swallowed hard. Rachael's car was now entirely inside and a ramp was lifted up by hydraulics to close the back of the trailer.

"They hide it from view, so the good people of the city won't realize what a street demon they owe their security to." Rachael looked down at the broken glass at her feet.

"Say kid, our people are clearing out, let's see who will give us a ride back to the station."

Rachael shrugged and walked towards the police vehicles.

At the station, Sanichiro Murayama, met them at the door. His Asian features matched his voice. "Sorry I couldn't stop the sedan from trying to take you out. They executed that right in the middle of my trace. I could have severed the connection but that would have been in the middle of program transfer. An incomplete program is more dangerous than—"

"Well done, Sanichiro. Did you get a trace on his accomplice?" Frank didn't break stride.

"Yes sir, Qualtine." He responded to Frank, but his eyes followed Rachael as she walked along between the two men without a word. "It was the Code Master. He was using a public data terminal, unauthorized access of course. As always, he was long gone by the time our officers got there."

"If anyone wants me, I'll be scraping paint off my bumper until quitting time."

"What will you, um, be doing after that?" Sanichiro asked.

"Visiting junk yards." Rachael didn't look at either of them.

Rachael pulled the distributor cap out from under the metal refuse that half buried it. Two spark plugs were still in it. They could be salvaged with some work. She turned it over lovingly and

4

looked at the corrosion on the bottom terminals. Too much rust.

She fumbled around in the pouch over her right shoulder and pulled out a socket. She snapped the socket onto a ratchet hanging from her belt and twisted the spark plugs out. The socket went back in the satchel, the spark plugs in her back pack, and the distributor cap, over her shoulder, back onto the trash heap.

Instead of her uniform, she now wore jeans with no knees and an old t-shirt that was cut to be sleeveless and midriff.

Rachael paused. Around the next metal rubbish pile she could hear movement. Anyone else would have dismissed it as a rat, but she smiled and sauntered around the edge of the pile.

There was a young man, about her age actually, on his hands and knees, carefully picking though the debris. He had shoulder length blonde hair, and if he hadn't been looking down she could have seen his rich blue eyes. He also wore jeans and a t-shirt, but his were still whole. A collection of four oddly-cut metal pieces were set deliberately on a dirty handkerchief besides him.

"Looks like you've found parts to a transmission, Chris," Rachael said.

"Oh, hi." He sat back on his heels and mopped his forehead, smearing it with dirt and rust. "There's not enough here to be worth anything, but I should be able to use them to put together one I've got at home."

"You've got a trans at home?" Rachael sat down on a cube that had once been the frame of a car.

"Yeah. These should be what I need to put a second together."

"Two rebuilt transmissions? Those will look impressive on your shelves."

"They would look better under hoods."

"Yeah," Rachael closed her eyes and nodded, "But real cars are outlawed by the emissions laws."

"That doesn't stop the badges from using them!"

Rachael choked and her eyes shot open, "I'm sure the police aren't all bad."

"Could have fooled me." Chris snorted and brushed his blonde hair out of his face.

Rachael cleared her throat, "I hear the museum has an exhibit of engine parts on display. Would you like to, um..."

"Yes. How's noon Saturday?"

"Wonderful!" her eyes dropped, "But, I can't guarantee my

work won't call me away at the last minute."

"We've talked a lot about cars, but not each other. What do you do for a living?"

She hesitated, "I operate delicate equipment, for one of the government offices. And you?"

"Unemployed, three months now."

"Oh, that's since I've known you. Why didn't you say something?"

Chris shrugged, "What could you have done? The only thing I'm qualified to do other than flip burgers is rebuild antiques."

"Anything I can do for you?"

"Well, I really came here looking for an ignition switch. If you see one, could you give me a holler?"

Rachael swung her backpack around in front of her and rummaged around in it. Down at the bottom, right next to the spark plugs was an ignition switch, the key fused to it with corrosion. She handed it to him. "I won't guarantee that it works."

He leapt to his feet and gently took it from her, his breath quickening.

"Why do you want this specific part?"

"Oh, I just I haven't gotten one of these to work yet." He spun around and scooped up the handkerchief with the transmission parts. As he trotted off he called back, "Thank you. See you Saturday."

"Frank," Rachael stuck her head though his office door, "where's that gas we ordered?"

Frank looked up, "Oh, you mean gasoline. I don't know. Why don't you call the lab? You know it wouldn't kill you to do a little of the paperwork yourself."

She turned around and walked back to the garage. The phone was affixed to the wall next to a work bench. Rather than dialing she spoke into the receiver, "Specialty Chemicals."

There was a brief burst of beeping on the phone line, and then ringing. "Nelson's Specialty Chemicals."

"This is Officer Rachael Kurman. I'm inquiring about an order of fossil fuel we placed with you."

"That's right. 20 gallons of high octane gasoline. I just finished mixing it up for you." The man on the other end of the line said, "The tanks are sitting on the back loading dock. Now that's strange."

"What?"

"The gasoline. I'm sure I wheeled it back here just ten minutes ago."

Rachael's phone hit the ground forgotten. She snapped the covers back on the battery on the work bench and raced it over to the open hood. Literally dropping it into position she grabbed a wrench and the nuts to attach the electrical leads to battery. That job completed, she closed the hood around the air intake.

"Frank, Get it in gear! We have an MVC!" She shouted into the radio as she leapt into the driver's seat.

"What are you taking about? There's been no report."

"Rachael, how did you get on the road?" It was Sanichiro on the radio.

"I haven't, now open the garage door for me."

"What makes you think she's on the road?" Frank asked.

"I just had a report of a loud smoking vehicle traveling faster than the grid set speed on Cherry Blossom Street."

Then there was a new voice on the radio, "Robbery reported at Nelson's Specialty Chemicals. We believe the suspect is using a manual vehicle, MV response team dispatch."

Rachael already had the engine revving, "You heard the man. Frank, get over here. Sanichiro, open the blasted door."

Sitting down in the passenger seat Frank asked, "How did you know?"

"The thief stole fuel," Rachael said, driving out of the garage before Frank could get his door closed.

"Could have been an arson."

"Call me an optimist."

"You're scaring me." Frank said buckling himself in, "You shouldn't be ecstatic when you respond to a call."

"I love to drive." She shifted into second gear. "It's just been decided the only time I get to drive is when a crime's been committed."

"I don't get it. You were born well after computerized cars were the norm. Why do you love the old polluters so much?"

"I think I was born liking them." Third gear. "Like most kids I took apart my toys to see how they worked. Unlike most kids I could put them back together. Then it was models. Alcohol powered models, methane, propane."

"Those are all reasonably clean, why do love the cars that

came close to destroying the environment?"

Rachael laughed, "When life first appeared on this planet oxygen was lethal to it, but those microorganisms sprayed it into the air like there was no tomorrow. At the same time they pulled stuff out of the air that turned into petroleum. I'm just undoing the damage our ancestors did."

"But the primordial soup prepared the world for higher forms of life."

"Scared who I'm preparing the world for?" Fourth gear.

"You're not worried about the children?"

"The very old and the very young are always the first to die."

"How can you be so cold?"

"Cold?" She turned and gave him a pained look. "Cold is the society that tells me I can't do the only thing I love. Cold is the classmates who wouldn't talk to me except to tease me because I didn't have the same interests as them. Cold is the partner who recommends psychiatric evaluation on every performance review!"

"The road! Watch the road!"

Rachael looked ahead again. She was in the wrong lane, driving towards oncoming traffic, but the roads were clear. She moved back into her own lane and muttered, "Thank you, Sanichiro."

"Hey, no problem. Funny thing, there's been no gird attacks yet."

"No computer fighting?" Cherry Blossom Street had just come into view, "You mean this is a real, old fashioned car chase? East or West?"

"Yeah, really old fashioned. West."

The car rounded the corner and headed West on Cheery Blossom Street. Electronic cars idled along the sided of the road. Several blocks ahead, something was smoking in the middle of the road. Rachael's car covered the distance in a handful of seconds, but the source of the smoke was still five blocks ahead of her.

"I don't believe it." Rachael beamed, "Someone actually got a gas powered car back on the road!"

She pushed the accelerator into the floor. Overdrive. Moving closer to the fleeing vehicle she could see its primary color was junkyard rust. The windows were all present and tinted black. It was smaller than Rachael's car, having only two doors, and probably no back seat. The trunk cover was missing, revealing the four stolen gas containers. The whole frame shook and rattled and the exhaust pipe continuously backfired.

"Isn't it beautiful?"

"And you wonder why I recommend they put you in therapy."

The rusty criminal veered down a side street. Rachael hit the brakes and spun the wheel. The wheels squealed and the car slid sideways onto the sidewalk, sideswiping an ice-cream cart the proprietor had just vacated.

"Great, we're going to hear about that damage claim."

"Bill the criminal."

"He just turned left," the radio crackled.

"I know that, I can see him!" She followed around turn, at a lower speed this time.

"Sanichiro, any idea's where he's headed?" Frank asked.

"No doubt, sir. He's making for the Deadlands."

"Where?"

"He means the Forgotten City," Rachael said and sped up again.

"Could either one of you speak English?"

"The hundred square blocks labeled 'unpatrolable' around the old park on the squad room map." Rachael explained. "We have to catch him before he gets there."

"Are the gangs really that bad?"

"Not at all. Actually it has some of the better junk in the city."

"Then why do we have to catch him before he gets there?"

"Because it's a labyrinth. Squatter towns, rivers flowing across roads, gang built walls. It's a driving nightmare: too many places to hide."

The Forgotten City now loomed ahead of them. It had skyscrapers just like the surrounding area, but there were no windows left in them, and no electricity.

The getaway vehicle sped up.

"On the open road I would have outpaced this guy a mile back! But with all the twist and turns..."

The mystery car turned right, but rather than disappearing behind a building, it could be seen through a forest of closed umbrellas, an open air cafe. Rachael turned sharp, jumping the curb and plowing though the empty tables.

"Where are you? I can't see you on the grid map," Sanichiro

came over the radio. "What the...?"

"Stop this car, Officer Kurman! You can't drive through restaurants."

"Did Frank just say 'though restaurants?'" The surprise in Sanichiro's voice was replaced by shock.

"It was a shortcut I had to take to catch up with the perpetrator. Besides it's not personal. That cafe we just went through is the only place you can get a decent sandwich near the South Heap."

"You're going to get suspended for this," Frank chastised.

"Okay, you can drive while I'm suspended."

"Er, well..."

The mystery car turned left into the Forgotten City. The Deadlands were ringed in by a broken-down police barricade that hadn't been manned in over a decade. It was the middle of the day, but somehow the sky or even the very air got darker as they passed though a "gate" in the wall of rubble stretching between the buildings. The pavement was cracked and missing entirely in some places. Ahead a squatter camp scattered into the surrounding buildings at the approach of the two roaring monsters.

The rusty car swerved around one of the campfires and dropped into a pothole. It emerged from the ditch with a bounce. One of the cans tumbled out of the back of the vehicle. It fell, hit the pavement and rolled. Rolled backwards, rolled towards the fire.

Rachael aimed down an alley and threw on the brakes.

"Why..." Frank was cut off by an explosion.

"What was that?" Sanichiro crackled over the radio.

"The sound of fate laughing at us," Rachael responded.

"We've lost him. Sanichiro, could you tell the pickup crew where we are? Rachael, pull back onto the road so they can pick us up."

Rachael grabbed the stick and put the car in first. "Right. This is too much! I had that guy outclassed eight ways to Sunday and luck stopped me from catching him."

"Don't blame yourself, you did more than everything you could to catch him."

"Next time, he's mine."

"What makes you so sure there will be a next time?"

"He has about fifteen gallons of gas and a criminal disposition. He'll strike again."

"Manual Vehicle Crime in progress. Manual Vehicle Unit please respond," The station intercom boomed. "Repeat, MVC in progress MV Unit please respond."

Rachael sat up and pushed the hair out of her face. She had been sleeping on an old bench seat in the back of the garage. Listlessly she picked her gun up off the floor and put it in her under arm hustler.

"Suspect using petroleum powered vehicle."

She sprang to her feet. A tall, blonde police woman sprinted through the door, "Officer Qualtine isn't on duty right now, so I'll be riding with you."

"Fine, strap in," Rachael said, sitting down and pumping the gas pedal.

The engine started with a roar. The new officer jumped in her seat. The garage door opened. It was dark outside, must be night. Rachael turned on the lights as the car sped up onto the road.

"Um, excuse me, Officer Kurman," the woman hesitated. "You're not in uniform."

Rachael looked down. The blue pants and the black undershirt were both part of the uniform but the shirt with her badge was back in the garage, "If there's anything left of this guy when I'm done with him, you make the arrest."

"The suspect is currently on Stone Ridge Road." Sanichiro yawned into the radio.

"Ooh, that's an expensive neighborhood. I wonder what it's like living in those big beautiful houses."

Rachael looked at her temporary partner with disbelief. "Who exactly are you?"

"Officer Shelly Dunnun. I've just finished the training course." She smiled.

"What are you doing on the MV unit?" Second gear.

"They said it was mostly paperwork, so sounded like a good, safe way to start my career in public service. Who drives when you're off duty?"

"No one. The only two drivers left in this city are me and the jerk on Ridge Road." Third gear. "Sanichiro, should I take the highway or cut up Main Street?"

"Doesn't matter, there's still no activity on the grid, I can run blocking for you wherever."

"Grid speed is higher on the highway," Shelly commented.

"I'm more worried about pedestrians, but highway it is." Fourth gear.

Shelly swallowed hard and clutched the arm rest, "Um, heh heh. How fast does this car travel?"

"I don't know, never got the speedometer calibrated."

"On open road she can make it between mile markers in thirty seconds on a good day, but I think she has burst higher than that." Sanichiro commented over the radio.

As the car angled on to the on ramp Rachael shifted into overdrive. Minutes passed quietly on the highway. Rachael sat back from the wheel slightly, Sanichiro started to whistle absently as he kept all vehicles out of the right lane, and Shelly sweated.

Rachael took her foot of the gas as she veered down the off ramp. She was halfway down when Sanichiro came over the radio. "You're practically on top of him."

Just then, the rusty sports car passed the bottom of the exit ramp. Rachael's accelerator went though the floor. The police car hit the concrete curb that separates the right and left turning traffic, and leapt into the air.

"I don't want to die!" Shelly screamed.

"What the...?" Rachael said as she got her first good look at the car.

"What 'What the...?'" Sanichiro asked.

"This isn't the same car as last time. I mean it is the same car, but there's less smoke, the frame doesn't shake as much and it hasn't backfired yet."

"So what?" Shelly screeched, hysterical tears rolling down her cheeks.

"So what. This guy didn't find his car, he rebuilt it and now he's tuned it."

"Like a musical instrument?" Sanichiro again.

"A well tuned engine is music."

The criminal car skidded around a hard right turn. Rachael followed, only she turned harder, faster, and skidded farther.

"What is this idiot doing?"

"What do you mean Sanichiro?"

"Before the next intersection this road has a drawbridge on it, for the yachts." Sanichiro spoke. "I'll raise the bridge and you'll have him trapped."

"Soon I'll have you, my worthy foe."

"Cou–could you stop laughing like that?" Shelly asked. "You're scaring me."

"Aren't you more worried about that brick wall in front of us?"

"Where?" Shelly's head snapped back around to face forward. Rachael laughed harder.

The street twisted and turned around the mansions. The road made a hairpin turn to the left, dropping down to follow along the contour of the hill. The drawbridge could be seen about half a mile ahead. As Sanichiro had promised, the two halves of the bridge angled up instead of meeting in the middle.

Instead of trying to double back, the fleeing car sped up.

"Oh, two can play at that game." Rachael pushed the gas to the floor and her hand dropped to the stick shift, thumb hovering over the nitro switch. Then her thumb stopped just hovering. Shelly's scream was drowned out by the scream of the engine.

The police car closed quickly on the other. With a jolt, both vehicles ran up on to the drawbridge, Rachael only slightly behind the target. Suddenly the other car swerved into the lane for oncoming traffic and the brake lights flashed.

Rachael's jaw dropped as she stared at the car, her head following it until she was looking over her shoulder. The escaper was now at a dead stop near the end of the drawbridge, meaning Rachael was...

The car landed on the other side, much harder than when it had jumped the curb. Rachael wrestled with the wheel to keep from going over the side of the bridge. She threw the car out of gear and stood on the brakes. Shelly's eyes were closed and she was covering her head with her hands crying hysterically.

The car skidded sideways and came to a stop. It rocked up onto the two leading wheels, then fell back onto all four.

"Get that bridge down now!"

"I can't! Someone's cut the power."

Rachael leapt out of the car and ran to the railing where the ground dropped ten feet down to the docks. By the street lights, she could see the silhouette of the other car. A shadowy figure stood besides the small building housing the bridge motor.

Rachael drew her gun and tightened the trigger; the hammer came back. She aimed at the person across the river gap. Then she relaxed and the hammer came down, uncocked.

13

"I won't gun you down in the dark. This is between two drivers, and that's the way we will settle it."

She reholstered her sidearm and went back to the car. As Rachael approached, the passenger door opened and Shelly rolled out on to the ground. She crawled to the gutter, ruining the knees of her nylons on the asphalt, then vomited.

Rachael reached in the open door and grabbed the radio. "Any chance of getting around the bridge and catching up with him?"

"Not really. He's making good time for the Deadlands."

"Right, send out the pickup crew then."

"I don't hear whimpering anymore. Did your new partner pass out?"

Rachael looked over. Shelly was curled up into a fetal position on the road, "Not quite."

After a couple minutes, the drawbridge began to hum and the two sides came down and joined together. Headlights from a grid car shined across the bridge as the vehicle rolled forward. The electric minivan came to where the road was blocked by the gas powered car and Frank got out.

"That was fast. You live around here?" Rachael asked.

"Like I could afford to. Sanichiro contacted me fifteen minutes ago. After he woke me up at this insane hour he insisted that I finished getting dressed in the car while he directed the car towards the chase route."

"Why weren't you at the station?"

"Believe it or not, I like to spend some time with my family." He walked over to the squad car, "Sanichiro, can the investigation of the robbery site wait until after dawn? Preferably after breakfast?"

"The victim has already mentioned several times the large contributions he makes to the Policeman's Ball."

"That means 'no.' Alright. I'll take whoever rode with you up to... aw, man. They stuck Shelly with you?"

"Hey, you weren't around." Rachael sat down on the still warm hood.

"But she doesn't have the nerves to ride with you."

"Come on, I've talked to your wife."

"What's that supposed to mean?"

"Your church attendance was spotty at best before you were assigned to MVU, and you haven't missed a week since you started riding with me. Who doesn't have the nerves to keep up with me?"

Shelly staggered over to them, "If it's all the same to you, sir, I'd like to wait a while longer before getting back into a vehicle."

"So we'll all stay here until the pickup squad arrives?"

"Not necessary. I'll go with Frank." Rachael took Shelly by the arm and pulled her back to the driver side door.

"The pick up squad will need the car in neutral, okay? The parking brake is on; to release the brake and put the car in neutral, pull this switch. Not this one," She indicated the switch to open the hood, "but this one."

Shelly nodded weakly.

"Right, now let's go see what my friend stole."

A man in an expensive robe sipped nervously at glass of scotch as the butler brought in Officers Kurman and Qualtine, "A plainclothes detective and a SWAT team member stripped down for action? Is that all the department cared to send?"

"We are the Manual Vehicle Unit," Rachael threw back her shoulders, "Since the culprit has revived one of the true masters of the roads, this is our jurisdiction."

"Very well," the house's owner growled. "I hope you will treat this case with the attention it deserves. The objects stolen are literally irreplaceable."

"Yes, well that's the next item of business." Frank pulled out his pocket computer, "The butler told us you are Richard Highton."

"Sir Richard Highton."

Frank made the correction. "Have you had time to ascertain what was stolen?"

"Yes, it wasn't bloody difficult. The plaques on the smashed cases say exactly what was stolen."

"May we see these broken cases?" Frank asked.

"I damn well wouldn't have called the police out here in the middle of the night, just to tell them they can't see the crime scene! Follow me." Sir Highton stormed towards the door.

Frank turned to follow. Rachael stood motionless until Sir Highton stomped past. Like a coiled snake, her left arm struck out and grabbed his oriental silk collar. With a snap and a yank she took him from his tall stature to looking up to make eye contact.

The glass he was holding shattered when it hit the floor.

For a moment, he was too shocked to be outraged. Rachael used that time to draw a switch blade. There was an ominous click and she touched the point to his Adam's apple, "Either you cut out this attitude, or I'm going to cut it out of you."

"How dare you! With a snap of my fingers I could have your badge as a paper weight!"

"You could, but then you'd never get your collection back." Rachael smiled at him psychotically, "You see, I'm the only one who can catch your burglar."

"You common bitch..." he stopped. A single drop of blood slid down the blade.

Frank cleared his throat, "Sir Highton, may we please examine the site of the break in?"

"Yes, certainly," he stood up and rubbed his neck. "If you two distinguished public servants would follow me, the lounge is this way."

While he was still watching her, Rachael licked the blood off the knife and folded it back into the handle.

In an outer wall of the lounge there had probably been glass doors before tonight. Now there was a 10-foot gaping hole with only bits of glass left clinging to the top and sides. The wall opposite the break-in had shelves, real books, and the door out to the hall. The wall on the right had unbroken cases containing antique weapons and coins. The left wall was a collection of broken glass and intact display cases. The unopened cabinet contained automotive parts.

Rachael began reading the labels on the empty cabinets, half to Frank, half to herself, "Water pump, fuel injector," she skipped an intact case with a windshield wiper mechanism, "pistons..."

"Can you detect any pattern in what he took and left?"

"None whatsoever. The most valuable piece is the missing carburetor, but the next best, the radiator, is still there."

"You know nothing about cars." Rachael called over her shoulder.

"I beg your pardon."

"That supposedly valuable radiator has a stress line all the way down. If you tried to use it, it would split open like a piñata."

"What difference does that make? If you used any of these parts they would wear out into worthless scrap."

16

Rachael turned around, her head bowed slightly. She looked up without moving her head, "How can you not get it? He drove though the side of your house. He puts these precious antiques back where they belong, in engines."

"But the perpetrator already has a working vehicle." Frank pointed out.

"There is a difference between an engine running and an engine roaring. Everything stolen will make him faster, more powerful, and more difficult to catch." She turned back around and pointed, "Look, racks for nearly twenty pistons, only eight missing from the large end. If you inventory I'm sure you'll find they are all the same size. He's probably boring out his cylinders right now."

"You have to stop him before he can put those parts under stress."

Rachael shook her head, "If I were you I'd collect the insurance and try to forget about it. We'll catch him but he may burn out his engine in the process."

The chief of police straightened up behind his desk, "You can't be serious."

"Why not?" Rachael stuck out her chin, "I can't be on duty twenty-four hours a day. You need a second driver. He just might join if offered full amnesty."

"After the way he's torn up this town and humiliated us – humiliated you."

"All the more reason to have him on our side. And I have not been humiliated! The first time was pure luck; the second I made the jump he couldn't."

"It amounts to the same thing. You've done almost as much damage as the culprit, and he's still on the loose."

"This is a way to prevent more damage. Don't make me mangle the car or the driver."

"Why the sudden concern for your victims? The last suspect you caught had seven broken bones and a mild conclusion. Is this antique freak a friend of yours?"

"He knows what a real car is. Which is more than you can say!"

"Why you, you had better watch it or—"

"Or what?" Rachael now had her hands on his desk leaning forward and glaring down at the police chief, "If you could afford to fire me you already would have."

The chief's face was now bright red between his graying hair and mustache. His voice cracked in hysteria, "Get out of my office!"

Rachael turned and laughed, "Yep, that's the only punishment you have."

As she sauntered out, Frank lingered in the office, "I'll have a word with her. I'm sorry for her behavior."

"You don't have to apologize," He fished in his desk for antacids, "We knew she was headstrong when we accepted her application."

"Why did she join?"

"Some fool reporter posted an article about a junker rusting away in storage."

Rachael squatted down to look into the museum case at eye level, she smiled and giggled, "Spark plugs."

"Actually I believe those are glow plugs." Chris offered, looking over her shoulder, "For diesel engines."

"Oh, of course," she blushed up at him.

She touched the glass lightly, "They've all been covered with a preserving lacquer. They'll last a long time, but you can't use them. They are like the bones in the other room, dead."

"Not all cars are dead," he patted her on the shoulder, "even if the badges have them."

Rachael's mouth opened slightly the lower lip quivering. Her eyes misted but no words left her throat. She was glad her back was to Chris.

Perhaps he saw her reflection in the glass because he stepped back and offered her a hand to stand. She put her hand in his and they both froze, Chris with a goofy smile, his hair falling across his face, Rachael wide-eyed and opened mouthed.

"You want to go for a drive?"

"I do," Rachael answered in a dream. The when her head was back on her shoulders she asked, "What?"

Chris jerked his thumb towards a dated arcade game labeled "Road Race" with a smear of blood red paint turning the 'c' into a 'g.' A group of early teens with ridiculous hair cuts and florescent face paint were vacating it, proud of completing the easiest track.

"Ladies first."

Rachael sat down on the game's seat and took off Chris' denim jacket, the museum had been too cold for her homemade tank top. She spun to face the controls. It was set up like an automatic with the gear shift in the floor. An unassuming button on the steering wheel was labeled 'Turbo.' She tried the pedals. There should have been more resistance in the brake and less in the gas.

The list of tracks appeared and before she thought, Rachael cranked the wheel to the expert course and tapped the turbo button. The road appeared on the screen with a red dot suspended in mid air. She pressed both pedals to the floor and shifted into overdrive. The dot turned yellow, then green. The foot over the brake shot up. After some initial overcorrection, sending some of the phantom competitors spinning off into the electric desert, Rachael handled the controls without incident and without letting up on the gas.

Rachael's fictitious car came to a hairpin turn, similar to the turn on Stone Ridge Road. She spun the wheel exactly as she had that night. The screen scrolled around 180 degrees, then another 180 degrees. The image rolled over upside down and red letters flashed on the screen reading "Game Over."

"That's not what real cars do. Uh, er. I mean this stupid computer can't possibly simulate what driving is really like. Here, your turn."

Chris' driving style was much like Rachael's, down to spinning out of control on the same curve. "Yeah, I don't think this is what driving is really like."

Just beneath the steps of the museum, Chris stopped and turned to her. He opened his mouth and after an awkward moment of no words coming out, he closed it and signaled for her to wait with his left pointer finger. From his back pocket he drew a hood ornament. Unlike most of the junk in the Forgotten City the paint and chrome were still intact. "I wanted to thank you for the ignition switch. It's not much, but..."

Rachael threw her arms around him and kissed him. She had only meant for it to be a quick kiss but neither of them was in a hurry to turn loose. When they parted it was only by an inch or so. She kept her arms around his neck and he kept his hands on her lower back.

"What was that for?"

"I don't know." Rachael said, "I'm sorry."

"That's okay. Just warn me next time so I can take a deep breath. You almost killed me."

"You almost killed me!" The latest manual vehicle criminal screeched as Rachael half led, half dragged him out of the mangled electric car. The engine was wrapped around a light post she had nudged the car over enough to hit.

"You've got a lot of nerve wasting my time when there is a real driver out there somewhere." She dropped, or threw, him to the pavement and stuck the barrel of her pistol in the base of his skull, "Now, put your hands behind your back."

"Officer Kurman, that is not proper arrest procedure." Frank rebuked.

Rachael snapped the hand cuffs on the suspect and sat down on his back, reholstering her weapon, "Let's see how does that go? You have the right to remain silent…"

"Rachael, you're out of control. The chief won't fire you, but one more incident like that, and I will have to go over his head."

"Relax, Frank. I'm going to resign after I catch The Driver." Rachael said as she affixed her new hood ornament to its proper place.

"What?"

"There are many people who don't like the police. I don't want to be part of that anymore."

"Admittedly, your resignation would improve our image, but you realize the car stays with the department."

"I know. I'll even leave all the parts I salvaged, except this," she said, cradling the hood ornament.

Sanichiro staggered into the garage and dropped into a bucket seat by the door. "That punk you hauled in by his nose ring made a positive I.D. on the Code Master as his accomplice. I tell you, that guy has this figured out, selling hacking services to MVCs he takes virtually no risks and gets huge payoffs. Rumor is, he selling his programs to small timers when he's finished with them. Personally he's been linked to over three dozen manual vehicle crimes, six illicit funds transfers, and the time I had to shut down the governor's limo to keep it form going off the bridge.

I got a medal for that, you know."

"The governor gave it to you personally, didn't he?" Rachael asked without much interest.

"You remember?"

"I remember having to wear the dress uniform."

"I remember," Frank said, but Sanichiro didn't hear him. The technician was staring at Rachael with a hurt expression.

Rachael was looking over some of the accursed paper work, still on real paper, and sipping a morning coffee when her computer mailbox beeped. She checked it. It had an anonymous sender and was addressed not to an individual, but to the MVU, which almost assured it was a complaint. She read the message anyway.

`"Interstate 14 West bound, Galleon on-ramp petroleum car seen."`

It would have been easier to use the phone, but Rachael stood up and yelled across the squad room, though an open door to the computer room, "Sanichiro, did you read this?"

Her phone rang and she picked it up, it was Sanichiro. "Yes. The Code Master is running a complex traffic control pattern on I-14 West. Get to the car. I'll send Frank out."

In the computer room Sanichiro had his right hand typing on one keyboard, his left on another. His eyes darted back and forth between the two screens. Without missing a keystroke on either hand he spoke into the phone headset, "Hang up. Dial: Qualtine."

The left-hand computer scanned the current duty roster and found almost instantly that Shelly Dunnun was currently assigned to the front desk.

"Frank Qualtine speaking."

"Frank, get to the car. It's Rachael's friend, and the Code Master. Hang up. Dial: front desk."

He activated patrol car 152 and sent it to the front of the building.

"Hello, this is the Police Department, front desk. May I help you?"

"Shelly, get in the squad car that just pulled up to the front door. I'll explain over the radio. Hang up."

His right hand, which was currently stopping the Code Master form blocking an on ramp, didn't stop while his left hand took a break from controlling the squad car. While he was waiting for confirmation that Shelly had entered the vehicle, his left hand switched on the police radio next to the computer.

"Who's ready?"

"We are." Frank sat down in the passenger seat just as Sanichiro asked.

Rachael was revving the engine wildly. The garage door opened as it was told to do by Sanichiro in his distant control room. Rachael found first gear like she had been born in the driver's seat.

"I am," Shelly's voice crackled over the radio.

"What does she have to do with this?" Frank asked, concerned.

"Mission brief: In addition to the tip, the I-14 computer's been hacked. The machines haven't finished analyzing the algorithms yet, but I know it's the Code Master. Instead of congesting the road, the program is clearing a path to the city limits. I'll try to route squad cars onto I-14 to keep the Code Master busy. Shelly is currently en route to the area the hack is coming from. I will adjust her course as more information becomes available."

"The hack only goes to the city limits?" Frank asked.

"Yeah, makes sense. That's where the Road Master Program turns cars over to the GPS server."

"I don't get it. He's using a hacker accomplice this time? Galleon ramp clear?"

"Yes and yes."

She sped up the ramp and scanned for vehicles. There was one. The silhouette was the same as the car she had chased before but it was no longer rust red; now the color was gloss black. It was in the right-hand lane right next to her, matching her speed exactly. It shifted over allowing her to merge.

"Sideswipe him and finish it now!" Frank yelled.

"No. He tipped us off. This is a challenge. First one to the city limits wins." Overdrive.

"Rachael, get a grip! There are no more knights is shining armor or bouts for honor. Your job is to catch that criminal."

Rachael moved into the right lane, the black car faltered for a moment, then pulled next to her. An instant later it pulled ahead and Rachael could see the trunk was now in place. Not to be outdone, Rachael's gas pedal merged with the floor and the black car was leading by only half a length.

"There were never knights in shining armor. Honor is in the individual, not the era."

"What about the dishonor of dereliction of duty?"

"Lay off her. You need to drag this out as long as possible to keep the Code Master distracted."

The road curved to the right, Rachael took the turn wider than the black car. After a frantic moment of braking and then accelerating to keep from colliding, Rachael was in the lead on the left.

A police cruiser came up the on ramp ahead of them. At the top it stopped and backed down.

"Sanichiro, stay out of this!"

"Keep your perspective. The big fish is the Code Master. The car driver is a bonus if we can catch him."

Rachael reached down and grabbed the radio. With inhuman strength she ripped it out from under the dash and threw it in the back seat. When she looked up the black car was dead even. Frank had drawn his gun and was rolling down his window.

"What are you..." In her surprise she let up slightly on the gas. The black car crept ahead.

"You and Sanichiro are playing games," he aimed at the driver's window, "but I remember what this badge means."

He fired. The tinted glass window shattered. A man with shoulder length blonde hair shielded his face from the flying glass. In slow motion Rachael fell away from the other driver. A single question formed unasked on her lips, "Chris?"

The world was spinning.

"—oad! Watch the road!" Frank screamed.

Rachael recovered just in time to keep from going through the guardrail. The car continued to spin. She downshifted and ended the spin.

Ahead, the black car went hard to the left. It had to slow down to make the turn. Rachael shifted into fourth and continued to speed up around the turn. Ahead a large green and white sign read, "City limits. Thank you for visiting."

Kerchunk! Screech! Black smoke bellowed out of the hood. The police car jerked and rolled to a stop.

Frank looked around wildly. Rachael was resting her forehead on the steering wheel, tears forming at the corners of her closed eyes, "I missed overdrive, that was reverse."

"So why aren't we going backwards?"

"The transmission is not just broken, it's destroyed," Rachael croaked.

Just past the city limits sign the black car turned sideways across the road and stopped. Even though the window was gone, the driver was hidden in the dark interior. Then the car straightened out and sped down the highway.

Shelly pulled the laptop computer away from the data terminal and folded it closed.

"Give that back, broad." The overweight, balding man at the terminal leapt up with surprising speed.

"I'm sorry mister Code Master, sir. You are under arrest and this is evidence."

He pulled out a small revolver and stuck it in her face.

An entire SWAT team cascaded down the subway stairs, leaping over the turnstile like a breaking wave of blue uniforms, gray armor, and black guns, "Everybody down!"

Most people complied with a scream. Shelly and the Code Master were left standing alone.

"One more move and the skirt loses her pretty head."

The SWAT froze in their tracks, weapons pointed at the ground.

"Now give me that computer!"

Shelly held the computer up just in front of her chest. The Code Master made a grab for it. She swung the computer up, hitting his gun hand forcing it to point towards the ceiling. She kicked him in the groin then stepped forward, smashing the bottom of the computer into his face.

The Code Master staggered back and a SWAT dog pile formed on top of him. The battered hacker was led away and the computer was put in an evidence bag.

The SWAT commander came up to Shelly.

"Now I know why these skirts are slit so high. And I thought you boys just liked looking at my legs." Shelly put her right hand on her blonde pony tail, the left on her waist and stuck her hips out to the left, so the slit in the skirt rose higher than usual.

"Uh, they're nice too, but..." The young commander shook his head. "Good work. I've seen veteran officers lose their nerve with a gun in their face."

"Oh that wasn't scary. Riding in a manual car is scary."

"You're ManVic? Well, I've heard a lot of mud slung your direction, but now that I've seen you in action, you're a credit to the Department."

It took the pickup squad several hours to get Rachael and Frank. Rachael said nothing while waiting, or during the ride back to the station. Police Headquarters was abuzz with activity when they arrived. A mob had formed calling for the Code Master to be brought to swift and harsh justice. A mass of reporters swarmed anyone claiming membership in the MVU. Sanichiro was answering questions while loosing a search program on an e-mail calling for the immediate release of the Code Master 'or else.' Shelly had a flower tucked behind each ear and one through her collar buttonhole. Every two minutes she moved the rest of the bouquet to a different spot on her desk and reread the card from the SWAT commander.

The chief met them at the door with handshakes, "Good work. I have three cities wanting to form their own MVUs. How quickly can you start training drivers?"

Rachael moved past without a word.

"Officer Kurman, a grateful citizen dropped this off for you a couple of minutes ago." Someone handed her a heavy cardboard box.

She set it on a near by table and numbly flipped out the switch blade. She cut it open. There was a note on top of the packing material. "Your picture is all over the news. Why didn't you tell me you were a police officer? Sorry I kept calling you badges. I found a job in another city so I won't see you for a long time. Here is a parting present for you. I don't need two transmissions. – Chris."

Rachael fell to her knees and wept into her hands. Sanichiro put a comforting hand on her shoulder which she never felt. In the middle of the crowd she was completely alone.

Captain's Quarters

"The rest of the ship is secure! What's taking you so long?" Captain Yubitsa Lopez shouted to be heard over the gunfire.

"There are at least two guys holed up in the cabin at the end of this hallway," Butch responded. "And they've got a lot of ammunition!"

"I'll handle it. Kill the lights!"

Capt. Lopez moved the patch from her left eye to cover the right. One of these days she was going to get the normal-vision setting fixed in her cybernetic eye. Until then, she had to keep either it or her flesh eye covered or else seeing the world in overlapping views of true color and the thermalgraphic night vision would give her a splitting headache.

With the tinkling of broken light bulb shards falling to the floor, the blinding red haze dimmed and she could see the distinct body heat signatures of Butch and Willy. Butch's armored cybernetic skull showed up distinctly cooler than the rest of his body. The same was true for Willy's legs and eyes.

As soon as she could see, Capt. Lopez spirited around the corner as fast as possible in the tall heeled boots she insisted on wearing. The two sailors were making good use of the cover provided by the bulkhead. She could see only their arms and part of the faces in front of the blinding light streaming through the door. The sudden darkness in the hallway took the two men off guard and bought her a couple of seconds before they started firing again. That was enough time for her to close and lunge to the floor. She spun to land on her back. From that low, close vantage point she had a clear shot at the light in the room. With that light gone, the ship's interior was pitch black, unless you had thermovision.

"Close the door." The standing man fired at random into the darkness.

The kneeling man reached across the opening, feeling for the door. Yubitsa shot him square in the chest as he exposed himself. He gurgled on his way to the ground. She must have missed the heart and hit a lung.

The remaining sailor screamed as he shot. Capt. Lopez rolled over onto her belly and glided across the floor like a shark in shallow water, avoiding the stream of hot lead death flying above her. It was rather unsporting the way she got close enough to shoot almost straight up into his chest by way of his hip. He went down, still screaming.

Capt. Lopez stood and walked into the room, then dead-checked both men with a round to the forehead. That was the pirates' creed: no quarter given and none expected.

"All clear. Let's search the room. It's possible they were just holding out, but they might have been protecting something."

Thermographic was not a good way to search for swag; inanimate objects were difficult to discern and harder to identify.

Capt. Lopez flung open the locker. The woman hiding inside screamed. Yubitsa grabbed her by the collar and flung her into the middle of the room, then planted her heeled boot on the woman's stomach, "Nice hiding place, senorita, but nothing on a naval vessel smells as good as that lavender perfume you're wearing."

Blinding red light filled the room.

"Willy! How many times do I have to warn you about the flashlights?" Yubitsa shielded her left eye with her hand until she could get the patch back over it. The cyber eye didn't have lids, so she couldn't close it. Actually the circuits surrounding the optics filled the entire eye socket from her cheekbone to the brow. Having been covered, her right eye was already accustomed to the darkness.

"Sorry, Captain. But you said to search the room didn't you?"

"I've found what they were protecting."

In the light she could see the woman was wearing an ensign uniform. Her blonde hair was cropped short, in standard military style, unlike Yubitsa who had been letting hers grow out since the end of the war.

"Your ransom will make this whole raid worthwhile." Yubitsa smiled down at her.

"No one would pay for me."

"Look, those men gave their lives to protect you. If you tell us where to send the ransom demand, we'll set you free after we get paid. Or if you want to be stubborn, we might have to sell you to slavers to help make ends meet."

"I'm Ensign Sara Spearman, my serial number is—"

"Spearman? As in the Spearman ship yards?"

"Daddy said I needed to do a tour at sea to better understand the ships we build."

"Zip-tie her hands to keep her from swimming off, boys. Then take her to my quarters. I'm going to start planting the explosives."

Capt. Lopez stood by the hatch and watched in twisted satisfaction as the burning remains of the frigate lolled over and started to sink. She wanted to stay and watch until the last flames were doused in the brine, but a search party would be coming soon.

She climbed in and closed the hatch behind her, then slid the rest of the way down the ladder. Vlad gave her a sloppy salute, "Orders, Captain?"

"Take us down to 15 fathoms, silent mode. Set course for El Dorado."

The water pipes and pneumatic hoses lining the dim corridor presented enough of a temperature contrast that it would have been easier to navigate with her infrared vision, but Capt. Lopez knew the Wrath well enough that she could have found her way blindfolded and drunk.

When she opened the door to her bunk, Ensign Sara Spearman huddled in the far corner. "What are you going to do to me?"

Capt. Yubitsa Lopez extended the punching blade out of the back of her cybernetic right hand and bent down to cut the plastic zip tie binding the captive's hands. "Relax; you're safer in here than with my crew. Besides, I have a headache tonight."

Luxuries were scarce at sea and even scarcer on a submarine, but Yubitsa allowed herself a punching bag in her cabin. She stripped down to her underwear and began punching and kicking the bag. Modesty was one of the luxuries you didn't have at sea.

"Oh, dear," Sara regarded her with worried compassion. "There is so much chrome."

Yubitsa looked down. She didn't even notice anymore, or at least she tried not to notice: her right arm, her left leg, the patch of red, field-hospital issue, synthetic skin between her breasts, and of course her eye.

"Beats a peg-leg and a hook." She gave the bag a round house kick with her artificial leg to punctuate the point. "Every last one of them is a souvenir from your navy."

"Don't you ever get tired of being angry?"

"Sometimes." Yubitsa gave the bag a series of rapid jabs. "Then I remember the carpet bombing of Grandeur City."

"Your side started the carpet bombing tactics."

"We were desperate. After you seized or destroyed all of our off-shore oil rigs, brute force was our only chance to win the war before our fuel reserves ran out!"

"Those oil rigs were all in international waters; in clear violation of the drilling treaty."

"That treaty is over 200 years old. We've used all of the land reserves. Preventing us from expanding further out to sea was the same as a death sentence."

"But since the surrender at Kent, those drilling platforms have been rebuilt under joint operation. Your country is getting part of the oil. We've even donated billions to rebuild Grandeur."

"Those worthless landlubber politicians surrendered. I never did!"

"I get it," Sara gave a smug smile. "You don't hate us for fighting the war. You hate us for winning."

Yubitsa grabbed Sara by the wrist and yanked her to her feet. In the cramped quarters it was only one step until she was close enough to the door to open it and fling Sara out into the corridor, "Take your chances with the crew. See if I care!"

Capt. Lopez went back to beating on the punching bag, with even more aggression than before, trying to drown out the pounding and pleading coming from the door. If she had hated them for winning, everything would have been simple. The truth was, Yubitsa hated herself for losing.

She rubbed the patch of smooth plastic skin covering where they had implanted the blood pump. During any other era of history, she wouldn't have lived to see her country's disgrace. The round that destroyed her heart and lung would have killed her. But thanks to cybernetics, she continued to exist as a specter with no purpose other than revenging her own death.

"What have we got?" Capt. Lopez stormed onto the bridge. After last night's raid and before making port in El Dorado, she had been trying to get some sleep. But the alarm had ruined that possibility.

"We've got an echo on the sonar. It's a surface ship. Rabbit Ears say's it's a destroyer."

"No chance we'll outgun them in broad daylight. Kill the sonar, kill the engines."

Everyone sat and waited in the darkness. Capt. Lopez noticed Ensign Spearman standing at the back of the bridge. The Captian held her finger to her lips, then mimed slicing her throat with her thumb. Ensign Spearman nodded in response.

"Splashes in the water!" Rabbit Ears called out.

"Depth charges! Dive! We've got to get under the detonation level." Capt. Lopez vaulted into the captain's chair and braced herself for the shock of the explosives. "Man the torpedo tubes. Sonar, get me a lock on that ship."

The engines hummed to life, the bow of the Wrath dipped down and the submarine lurched forwards into the depths.

Dull booms resounded through the hull like the footsteps of a giant.

"Thirty degrees from the aft, port side, range 1000 yards." Butch called out the coordinates of the destroyer.

"Fire!"

The bursts of the depth charges grew louder. Yubitsa could feel them as much as hear them. The hull groaned with the passing blast waves. Each one would have made her heart stop, but her blood pump continued spinning with mechanical efficiency. Yet the fact that she heard the explosions meant they had missed. Just when she allowed herself to breath again, there was the sickening clank of metal on metal. There was only enough time to mutter a four letter word (which most of the crew did) before the force of the blast rocked the Wrath.

The jolt threw Capt. Lopez from her chair. The bridge erupted into chaos around her. The salty smell of brine mixed with the acrid metal smoke of electrical fires.

"We're taking on water. Blow the holding tanks." Vlad called out.

Capt. Lopez gathered herself and rushed the helmsman, slamming her shoulder into his head and knocking him out of his chair.

"If we surface we're dead."

"If we don't surface we're dead." Vlad moved for the helm himself.

The punching blade sprang out of the back of Capt. Lopez's hand, "Question my orders one more time and you die first!"

Vlad went for his own knife. Capt. Lopez charged before he could clear the sheath. She had been aiming her uppercut just below the sternum, so the blade would hit the liver, or maybe reach the heart, but Vlad's right forearm got in the way as drew. She spun to deliver a back-roundhouse-kick to his head but caught her heel on one of the low support struts on the bridge. Pain shot though the nerves of her flesh-and-blood leg.

In drawing his blade, Vlad's elbow struck her between the shoulder blades like a jackhammer. That was to be expected since his arms were hydraulic. Already off balance, Capt. Lopez flew face-first into the helm. She rolled on to her back and kicked both of her high heels into Vlad's chest. The pain probably would have dropped a lesser man, but against Vlad all it did was keep him far enough away that his stab skipped off her metallic thigh.

Capt. Lopez ripped off her eye patch and closed her natural eye. In infrared she could clearly see the cold blue tube protruding ever so slightly where the artificial arm merged with the flesh of the shoulder. She rolled forward and flung all of her body weight behind her punching blade as she stabbed the hose. Hot blood trickled out of the wound, but it was cold hydraulic fluid which sprayed her face and chest.

Vlad lunged at her again. But this time she reached up and caught his wrist. As Vlad strained to drive the knife into her flesh, he only caused hydraulic fluid to gush out of the wound. He tried to grab her with his functioning arm, but he was too slow. She stabbed him in the throat with her cyber-blade. It was a fatal wound. It shouldn't have been fatal in this day and age of modern medicine, but the cyber-surgery on the Wrath had been shamefully understocked ever since the Peace started.

Vlad backed away, gasping for air and sucking it in though the hole in his neck instead of his mouth. But Capt. Lopez didn't let mutineers off that easy. She followed, stabbing him in the gut, the face, anywhere she could find an opening. She drove the blade into his left hip and Vlad toppled. She fell on him like a she-wolf and punched her blade into the throat over and over.

Capt. Lopez wondered why she couldn't see hot blood

31

splattering everywhere. The shock of freezing cold brine against her legs reminded her they were taking on water.

Marcus had returned to the helm. In the infrared, his black skin glowed as red and yellow as her own.

"Bleed the tanks, don't blow them, and use the engines to hold us steady." She pointed her blade at him to punctuate the point. She could see hot blood covering the tip.

"Aye, Captain."

"Sonar, give me a target." Orders to run the pumps and plug the leaks were unnecessary. Capt. Lopez shuttered to think how many people had abandoned their battle stations when the blast had struck, "Sonar, I said..."

"Five degrees from aft on the starboard side, range 1500 yards."

"Fire!" Too late, Capt. Lopez realized, it hadn't been Butch's voice calling out the coordinates. She glared over. Butch was already growing cold. He must have fallen wrong; she had warned him that reinforced armored skull was too heavy for his neck. It was a woman hunched over the sonar screen. Aside from herself, there was only one other woman on the Wrath.

"If that torpedo misses..."

"Direct hit." The woman called out.

Capt. Lopez shoved Ensign Spearman out of the way and looked at the sonar for herself. She was forcibly reminded that she couldn't read the screen in infrared. Reluctantly, she opened her eye and held her hand over her artificial one so at least it was a uniform red haze superimposed over the world. She had heard the torpedo launch and now there wasn't a sonar echo for one. She'd have to take the ensign's word that it had struck. As she watched, the sonar echo of the destroyer shifted to the starboard side. Was it just an artifact of the motion of the Wrath? The next echo was a little further off center, and the next a little further still.

"They're breaking off to lick their wounds!"

A collective sign of relief shuttered through the Wrath. Capt. Lopez closed her eye and rubbed her temples. She'd need to find where she dropped the eye patch.

"Good work, men. Marcus, take us down another five fathoms, evasive maneuvers, but start meandering towards El Dorado."

"Anther five fathoms?" Marcus gave a pointed glace at the depth meter.

Capt. Lopez couldn't read it in the infrared, but she guessed they were already in the red. She kicked Vlad's body, "You want to make it 10?"

"Five fathoms. Aye, Captain."

Capt. Lopez dropped into the captain's chair and looked over at Ensign Spearman, "You realize by doing that, you've become a traitor and a pirate, don't you?"

"Those depth charges would have killed me the same as they would have killed you."

Yubitsa Lopez found Ensign Sara Spearman huddled in the corner of her Captain's quarters. Like everyone else onboard she was still soaking wet.

"Come on, it's time to make your ransom video."

The prisoner rose to her feet but did not look up. Capt. Lopez reached past her and pulled the blanket off the bed, "Wrap this around yourself. People are pretty easygoing in El Dorado, but they have an understandable hang-up about Navy personnel."

Ensign Spearman listlessly carried out the order.

"What are you waiting for? Let's get going!"

"Aren't you going to tie me up again?" She held out her wrists together.

"I'm the only one in this cesspit who sees you as something more than about an hour's worth of fun. If you're stupid enough to run away, you deserve what'll happen to you. But if you're a good girl, I'll buy you a real meal and a couple of drinks while we're in port."

Capt. Lopez struggled up the ladder to the hatch with a heavy duffle bag over her shoulder. The hot tropical sun beat down on the Wrath from high it the sky. The smell of brine competed with the stench of dead fish and spilled petroleum. Circling flocks of seagulls squawked overhead. The crumbling castles flanking the mouth of the harbor shone like gold as the sun glinted off the crushed shells in their sandstone blocks. Modern artillery pieces and radar arrays adorned the ramparts. The roofs of El Dorado were a uniform red tile, but the plaster sides of the buildings varied across the entire rainbow, dotted with elaborate graffiti.

A tent city no less colorful than the buildings filled the open square at the head of the docks. Yubitsa reached back and grabbed Sara's wrist as she threaded her way into the crowd. The hawkers called out in a variety of languages and broken English, advertising everything from the catch of the day to national secrets, both of which were probably stale by now.

Yubitsa caught the corner of a briefcase in her gut. A black man with a white beard wearing an ankle length robe and a turban had thrust the case at her to show off his array of handheld electronics. He rambled on in some language she didn't understand. She ignored him. The only thing she wondered about his wares was: which ones were stolen and which ones were fakes.

She had only forced her way two steps past the electronics hawker, when the cry, "Navy!" sounded out of the crowd behind her. Capt. Lopez spun to find the mass of people parting around her. The tattered corner of Ensign Spearman's blanket had gotten caught on the briefcase and pulled down. Ensign Spearman still wore it over her elbows like a shawl, but it was low enough to expose the rank insignias on her shoulders.

"Mother of the Fish!" Capt. Lopez dropped the duffle bag and drew her semiautomatic pistol as three towering thugs pushed their way past the first line of nervous spectators. Once they broke free of the crowd, she could see blue and yellow armbands on their left biceps. That was bad: the Wharf Rats gang was the official enforcers for the crime syndicates which ran El Dorado and the closest thing to there was to police in this corrupt town.

Rather than point her gun at them, Capt. Lopez pulled Ensign Spearman in front of her as a human shield and jammed her gun under the captive's chin. "She's my prize. I paid my docking tax. I can sell her anywhere I want."

"Go ahead and shoot. I say she's a spy." The trio moved to encircle the pair of women.

"Do you know who I am?" Capt. Lopez demanded.

"No, but your chest is big enough you could make more money selling yourself than with that navy chick." The ringleader was a giant Latino with a mane of black hair down to his elbows. If not for the scars adorning his bare arms, Capt. Lopez would have assumed that he was a full body cyborg as well chiseled as his chest muscles were.

Capt. Lopez was just glad they didn't know who she was. Being a small time pirate had its advantages. She fired on the ringleader. No time to aim, just blast away at the center of mass. The Wharf Rats, expecting an easy victory, hadn't drawn their weapons yet.

34

"Run," She shoved Ensign Spearman towards the sudden opening in the throng of people. Nothing like a little gunfire to break up a crowd. Capt. Lopez scooped up the duffle bag with her free hand and followed as fast as she could, cursing herself for her high heel boots.

The ringleader reached out to grab her. She swung the bag, aiming for his face. He ducked out of the way, but in doing so, gave Capt. Lopez enough space to escape. The thinning crowd gave her room to run, but it also gave the Wharf Rats a clean shot. Ensign Spearman was nowhere to be seen, making Capt. Lopez the only target. Lucky for her, the Wharf Rats were lousy shots.

Capt. Lopez dived into the first alley. The buildings would give her some immediate cover, but once the Wharf Rats made it to the mouth of the corridor, she'd have no place to dodge. The side street she had chosen wound its way up a hill. She sprinted up the worn stone stairs; in the tropical midday heat; carrying her heavy bag; while wearing high heels. She would have had a heart attack, if she had had a real heart instead of the blood pump whirring double speed in her chest. Even with an artificial lung, her breath was still labored. She couldn't fix the heat or take the time to remove her boots right now, but she dropped the bag.

She reached the top of the stairs, only to find that there was only a short landing before a flight of stairs even longer than the one she had just climbed. She almost didn't notice the figure beckoning her from the top of a crumbling yellow brick wall. It was Ensign Spearman.

Capt. Lopez lunged at the barrier and caught the top with one hand, Sara Spearman grabbed her other elbow and helped pull her over the wall. They crashed down together onto a carpet of bahia grass and weeds.

As Yubitsa Lopez lay panting for breath a hand clamped down over her mouth. So that Navy wench had lured her into a trap. Yubitsa should have shot her back there. She opened her eye, but the only person she could see was Sara, staring pensively at the wall. With the roaring of her own breath stifled, Yubitsa could hear running footsteps on the other side of the wall. The footsteps grew louder and closer and louder and closer and louder and closer. Then softer.

Sara didn't remove her hand until the footsteps had disappeared into bustle of the city.

Yubitsa sat up and gasped in a deep breath. The air was

35

heavy with the scent of flowers. The breath came out as a sigh. They had come over the back wall of a dilapidated garden. The brick outlines of the flowerbeds were barely visible beneath the layer of feral green. The only flowers were the wisteria vines climbing up the walls, and the dandelions. But they bloomed with laudable fervor, as if trying to make up for the rest of the garden.

"Why did you save me?" Yubitsa asked with her first controlled breath.

"I'm not sure. I just did. Why did you turn me loose?"

"Idiot, I can't ransom you if you're dead."

"You also can ransom me if I get away."

Yubitsa made a couple of over dramatic pants, to avoid the subject.

"Oh! You're bleeding."

"Nah, those hombres missed. The big guy must have splattered on me when I ran past."

Sara touched her back, ever so lightly and pain shot through Yubitsa like an electrical current. She was just glad the sweat covering her face would mask the tears. She spoke through clenched teeth, "Funny, I never even felt that one."

"I think your rib is broken. We need to get you to a doctor."

"Don't worry about it. That's the side with the cyber lung. Even if the bullet went straight through, it would keep working." That was a disturbing thought. As Yubitsa stood up, she unbuttoned her shirt and examined her right breast. No blood; the bullet hadn't gone straight through her.

"Lend me your blade."

Yubitsa held up her fist and sprang the knife out, "Even if I was dumb enough to give my hostage a weapon, it doesn't come off."

Sara grabbed the fist and guided it down to stab herself in the thigh. Yubitsa twisted around to see what was going on behind her. Sara hadn't stabbed herself; she was cutting off her right pant leg just below the pocket. After slicing the front of the pant leg, she tore the back to finish the job and wiggled the loose fabric down off her leg.

"What are you doing?"

Rather than answer, Sara reached into the pirate's still open shirt and wrapped the cloth around her back, in the act brushing her own breasts against those of her captor. The electric shock of pain ran through Yubitsa again as Sara laid the cloth over the bullet wound.

"Now breathe out as hard as you can."

Straining her wounded chest to exhale was painful, but it still hurt less than having Sara tie the impromptu bandage tight around her.

"That should at least slow the bleeding and help keep everything stationary until you get to a doctor."

"I'll have the Wrath's sawbones look at it later." Yubitsa rebuttoned her shirt, "Fewer questions that way."

Sara gave her an incredulous look.

"Okay, it's cheaper. All right? Look, I'm going back for the bag before those guys get smart and double back. Don't run off while I'm gone."

The only thing that surprised Yubitsa more than the fact that Sara was still there when she hauled herself back over the wall was the fresh rips on the shoulders and left breast of Sara's uniform. The ensign insignias lay in a pile at her feet.

"You said yourself, when I manned the sonar I became a traitor and a pirate. Right now I feel safer as a pirate than as an ensign."

"So Lopez, what can I do for you?" The man seated on the felt couch across the table from her wore a silk shirt and polyester pants. He crossed his legs to show off his alligator-skin boots. He was completely bald except for his goatee. Even his eyebrows had lines shaved into them.

"I need to shoot a video." Capt. Lopez jerked her thumb towards Sara Spearman.

He looked Spearman up and down like an antique dealer appraising a new item, "Man, you found a cute girl for the part. I'll cut you a discount if you let me be one of the guys who—"

"Get your mind out of the gutter, Renner! This is a ransom video."

"Lopez, only you're stupid enough to still be using your war name. How many times do I have to tell you: It's Duke now." He regained his composure and settled back into the center of the couch. "I'll negotiate the deal in exchange for a cut of the ransom, but I'm going to need something up front to start the film rolling. Of course if you're short on cash, with a body like yours, you could work it off. There's a lot of call for cyber-fetish right now."

"Shut up, Renner. I've got barter." Capt. Lopez wrestled a weighty cyberarm out of her now scuffed and tattered duffle bag and laid the cyber limb on the plastic table between them.

Sara Spearman sucked in her breath and stared at Capt. Lopez in wide-eyed horror.

"There is a little damage to the hydraulic line here at the shoulder, but other than that it's in perfect working condition."

Duke glanced over the arm, not nearly as thoroughly as he had inspected Spearman, "Okay we'll shoot your movie."

"I want them to be able to see she's unwounded. Get her a swimming suit. Something tiny but tasteful."

"You've come to the wrong place for tasteful." Duke laughed.

Sara Spearman's face blushed lobster red as she stood in the spotlights. The revealing bikini they had given her was so small that any sudden movement would have caused her to slip out of it. Her fists shook by her sides as she read the teleprompter. "I'm being held captive by Capt. Lopez of the Wrath. As you can see I'm uninjured. She has treated me well."

Yubitsa's head jerked. That wasn't part of the script she'd written, Sara had improvised that last line.

"When her terms are met, she will release me in a neutral port. However..." her voice faltered.

"Read it!" Duke ordered.

"...if you do not immediately pay the ransom, or if you attempt to rescue me, she will kill me on the spot."

"Now turn around." Yubitsa called out.

For the first time Sara looked away from the teleprompter, "No!"

"You're showing him there are no wounds. Turn around or I'll give you some wounds to show off."

Sara shuffled around backwards. The t-back left even less to the imagination that the front of the bikini. Yubitsa gave a wolf-whistle. Sara splayed her left hand to cover her buttocks. The right fist remained clinched at her side.

Duke glanced at Yubitsa, "And cut! By the way Lopez, you didn't say in the script, what's the ransom?"

"One of those new Mako class subs."

"What makes you think this chick is worth a Spearman

Mako?"

"Daddy will never give you one of our Mako class."

Duke looked back and forth between the two women. "You got a prize here Lopez, but a Mako? That's brand new mil-spec hardware."

"That's just an opening demand. They'll offer you a ridiculous amount of money instead. Then make them double it."

"I like the sound of my cut of double ridiculous. Is there anything else I can do for you?"

Capt. Lopez looked at the cut and torn uniform lying next to the costume rack, "Give her some real clothes, and some shoes to match, while you're at it."

"You were a very good girl today. So like I promised, let's get some dinner."

The sun rode low in the sky and as the heat abated, even the side streets and back alleys swelled to near bursting with bustling crowds. Yubitsa reached back and grabbed Sara's right fist around the wrist to guide her through the throng of people. The stiletto heals she had been given forced Sara to walk with a stilted gait which made her breasts bounce in the oriental gown that clung to her like a film. The sides of the dress were slit so high the straps of the bikini she was still wearing underneath were visible over her hips.

Yubitsa slipped though a gap in the green, painted iron fence partitions delineating the territory of one of the open air bistros taking up valuable space on the cramped sidewalk. She sat down at a matching green-iron table.

She didn't even wait until the waiter had placed the menus on the table, "We'll have a couple of cold beers and two hamburgers: Well done. Raw flesh all tastes the same and I've had enough fish at sea that I want to know I'm eating beef."

"And how will you be paying?"

Yubitsa fished two boxes of 9 mm ammunition out of her bag.

"Barter again? Why can't you attack merchant vessels like normal pirates?" The young man scratched his brown hair.

"Just take the shells and give us some food."

"Not this time, we have enough of your junk already."

Sara slammed her fist on to the table to draw their

39

attention. She opened her hand and necklace spilled out, "We'll be having two steaks, well done like she said, and the best bottle of chilled red wine you have."

The young man picked up the necklace to examine it. It was a silver dolphin, studded with diamonds.

"Yes, Madam," he bowed, "I'll bring out some bread and cheese to get you started. What kind of dressing would you like on your salads?"

"Bleu cheese for mine, and for you, Captain?" She looked to Yubitsa, "Captain?"

"Ah... right, bleu cheese."

Yubitsa didn't speak again until the waiter had disappeared inside the building, "I'm not worthy to call myself a pirate that I didn't notice you were hiding that."

"Maybe if you worried more about money and less about vengence."

"So how long had you had your fist balled up like that?"

Sara's hand was still flushed red with blood from the exertion, except for a white spot in the palm where the necklace had pressed into her, "I had been wearing it until you made me change out of my uniform at the movie studio. Doesn't it upset you going places like that?"

"I'm a pirate. Scum doesn't bother me."

"You're still a woman."

Yubitsa locked gazes with Sara and the sarcastic retort died in her throat. It would have been several heartbeats before she found the words to speak, but with the blood pump spinning in her chest, Yubitsa didn't have a heartbeat to count the time, "I am a woman. Sometimes this job makes me wish I wasn't."

"Bring us up alongside her, nice and quiet," Capt. Lopez whispered the order. "Get read to board, men."

Sara was standing at her usual place at the back of the bridge of the Wrath. Capt. Lopez beckoned her to follow with a wiggle of her finger and led the hostage down the corridor to the Captain's bunk. The pirate still wore her signature tall heeled boots, but Sara had opted for bare feet instead. The Captain opened the door and motioned her captive inside, then leaned close to whisper in her ear, "I can't risk a valuable prize like you trying to run away or getting caught in the crossfire. So I'm going to have to lock you in."

Sara shifted to whisper in Yubitsa's ear, "Please come back safely."

Yubitsa jerked her head back and stared at Sara.

"I can't let myself out if you don't come back."

Capt. Lopez let out a breath she didn't realize she had been holding. She closed the hostage in her bunk and shoved a steel rod though the door wheel to prevent it from spinning. She moved the patch to cover her right eye. The pipes lining the corridors of the Wrath burst into a colorful infrared display. Time for vengence.

By the time she made it to the hatch, Willy and Marcus had already scurried up to the deck and lowered a rope ladder for the others. They must have also neutralized the deck guards, because the coast was clear. Capt. Lopez motioned those two to follow her, and moved to the door into the aft castle. The rest of the men fanned out to storm the ship.

The door to the aft castle was locked. That was unusual, but not unheard of. Capt. grabbed one of the small charges from her belt to blow the lock.

The world went blinding red. She could hear a sudden stampede on the tops of the fore and aft castles, "Throw down your weapons!"

She dropped the explosive and wrestled the patch back over her cybernetic eye. Spotlights glared down from the mast, fore castle and aft castle. Beyond the glare she could barely make out dozens of assault-rifle wielding forms lining the railings above her.

"Throw down your weapons and lie down with your hands behind your head!"

Explosions roared off the starboard side. They were shelling the Wrath at point-blank range.

"Sara!" Capt. Lopez sprinted to the side. Automatic fire erupted around her. She dove over the railing and flopped flat on her stomach with the metal clank of her cyber limbs on the hull of the Wrath. Already, flames licked through holes in the hull and the Wrath was listing over on its side. The heat of a new explosion washed over her.

Capt. Lopez scrambled over to the hatch and slid down the wall into the dark interior. A foot of water at the bottom broke her fall.

Capt. Lopez fought her way through the torrents to her quarters. She didn't remember having jammed the bar in the door wheel this tight. It wouldn't budge. Then she remembered the door-opener explosives on her belt. One of those bent the wheel and sent the bar ricocheting down the corridor.

Water was already covering the door. Capt. Lopez spun the wheel, straddled the door and lifted up with all of her strength. She could feel the muscles strain and fail in her flesh limbs, but she kept pulling with all of her cyber strength. A slurping sound signaled that the seal had broken. She fought the door until the edge stuck out above the rising water level. Free of the weight of the water, the door flew open. Yubitsa Lopez twisted her body to avoid the door and flung herself down the drain.

Sara was in an unconscious pile in the water pooling on the far wall. Bright red blood ran out from a gash on her temple. Yubitsa scooped Sara up over her shoulder. She used the punching bag anchor bolt as a step to reach up and pull herself out of the room.

It wasn't until she reached the hatch that Yubitsa started wondering if Sara might already be dead. Yubitsa ripped off her eye patch, tearing the band in her haste. Despite the freezing brine pouring in on them, Sara still glowed bright red. Yubitsa hadn't noticed before just how little that thin dress did to mask her body heat.

Yubitsa pulled herself and Sara out of the hatch and got a single breath of fresh air before the undertow of the sinking Wrath pulled her back down. She clenched the hem of Sara's dress in her teeth to free both her hands and swam with all of her might against the current. Her flesh limbs already suffering from pulled tendons burned with pain but she ignored them.

She burst out the surface. The corvette was a blinding mass of light in both the visible and infrared. She could hear whistles and orders sounding, but no gunfire. So her men hadn't lasted very long. The way discipline and morale had deteriorated since the war, she wasn't surprised. Spotlights raked back and forth across the waves.

Yubitsa spat out the dress hem and grabbed Sara to hold her head above the water, "Over here. Don't fire! I have a civilian."

Until they had been hauled up onto the deck, Yubitsa kept her arms locked around Sara. The riflemen encircling them were an overlapping blur of visible and infrared. She couldn't tell which were real and which were double vision illusions.

She laid Sara down on the boards and stepped away.

Soaking wet, Sara's dress was as transparent in the visible as the infrared. That tiny bikini she was still wearing underneath wasn't much, but it was better than nothing with all these sailors around.

Yubitsa didn't resist as they cranked her arms behind her and hand cuffed her writs.

A sailor knelt down over Sara, "She's alive."

"Get her to sickbay." The order sounded from somewhere.

The sailor wrapped his arms around her chest and lifted her, intentionally or unintentionally cupping her breasts in his hands in the act.

"Take your hands off her!" Yubitsa lunged forward. The butt of an assault rifle slammed into her gut. She bent over double, gagging. The next rifle butt landed on the back of her head.

Yubitsa had no idea how long it took to rouse herself from the state of nauseated half sleep, or how long she had been unconscious before that. Her hands were still handcuffed and they had bound her ankles together for good measure. She was lying on a cold metal floor that stank of human odor. The only good thing was that the hood over her head was thick enough to block out both visible and infrared.

Nor did she have any idea how long she lay there before she heard the door unlock and two guards dragged her away by her biceps. She didn't even have the fight left in her to yell obscenities at them. After traveling for what seemed like hours they dumped her on a carpeted floor.

Someone ripped off the hood, trying to take her hair with it. Her flesh eye, fully dilated from the extended darkness, was as worthless as her cybereye.

"Captain Yubitsa Lopez. Wanted dead or alive on multiple counts of piracy, murder, and let's not forget one very important kidnapping." The grizzled voice of an old fishing captain boomed from behind the dazzling lights.

"You also saved my daughter's life. So I'm willing to call it even. I'll even offer you a business deal. In addition to our shipyards, we have a fleet of freight haulers. Turning you loose to prey upon the fleets of rival corporations would be very profitable for both of us and with your established criminal record, no one would think to connect you to our company. The Navy owes me enough favors that I got them to hand you over before word of your capture got out. So, as far as the world knows, you're still at large."

As her flesh eye adjusted to the light, Yubitsa could make out the form of a desk in front of a picture window. A woman, probably his secretary was standing off to the right. She couldn't make out the face of the man in the chair; the entire world was painted over with infrared glare.

"Of course you'll have to cool your bloodlust; give up your obsession with military targets. Which is just common sense anyways. We'll install a corporate overseer on the ship to make sure you don't get out of line." Mr. Spearman continued, "We'll even feed you intelligence to hit one of our ships from time to time to prevent suspicion, and keep you well stocked. After all, a Mako is a difficult ship to keep in top fighting shape."

"Mako?"

"That is what you asked for in exchange for my daughter wasn't it? So the choice is yours: swing from the gallows as the last relic of that war, or find your place in the new peace."

It should have been an easy decision. But Yubitsa longed for the peace of death that cyberware had robbed her of. That's what she had been looking for in all of those fights. That's why she always targeted well armed naval vessels. The pirates' creed: no quarter given and none expected. But she had taken a prisoner and had allowed herself to be taken prisoner. Maybe it was time to change her perspective.

"I accept your terms."

The woman moved from beside the desk and approached her. Yubitsa squinted against the light, trying to make out her features. She saw a flash of cold blue. No, it was visible true blue; a cloth of some kind. The woman tied the bandana over Yubitsa's cyber eye and the red haze faded.

"I was hoping you'd agree." Now Yubitsa could see that it was Sara bending over her. She was properly attired in an unbuttoned khaki shirt with a low cut white undershirt beneath it. On her belt she carried a knife, handgun, flashlight, and several pouches. "I've already had them hang a punching bag in our quarters."

"*Our* quarters?"

Sara smiled and adjusted the matching blue bandana covering the gash where she had hit her head, "Daddy did tell you there would be a corporate overseer onboard."

Binary Angel

The two security guards sitting at the front desk of the Cybernetic Research Institute looked at each other, then down at their watches. They both wore well pressed green and tan uniforms with "CRI" embroidered in gold thread above their nametags. One of them, Daniel Wallace according to the nametag, grunted softly and stood up.

Scattered in throughout the lobby were half a dozen young businessmen typing on palmtop computers or mini-phones. Not coincidentally, Daniel approached the only female; a blond in a sharp, black pants-suit, lingering near the security desk.

"I'm sorry, Miss, but the building is closed. If you want to stay, I need to see a company ID."

"I have my ID right here." There was a dangerous edge to her voice Daniel must have missed, because he didn't even flinch as she quick-drew a 9mm auto-loader pistol. It was a small gun, designed more for concealablity than accuracy or power, but a three round burst of hollow-point ammunition to the face at point blank range was more than sufficient. Daniel was dead before he realized what was happening.

The guard behind the desk wasn't so lucky. He blanched and sat stunned for a heartbeat, then screamed and dove under the desk.

One of the businessmen pressed a button on the handle of his briefcase. The sides of the case fell away, revealing a submachine gun. He tossed the gun up to chest level and grabbed it by the grip, closing his finger around the trigger in the motion. Bullets strafed the reception desk erratically, ripping through the particle board. Blood started to leak out around the base stand.

"Move out boys! We're on a tight schedule." The woman called, ripping off her business coat, leaving only a black t-shirt stretched over a torso too well muscled to be anything but artificially constructed. The other 'businessmen' uncased their guns. The incursion team moved to the number-pad locked door in the south wall which led the research labs.

A small figure darted towards the security desk from the other side of the lobby. An oriental woman had been curled up asleep on one of the rows of bench seats. She wore a wrinkled security uniform with a skirt. Her brown eyes looked smaller than they actually were due to the lensing effect of her thick wire rim glasses. Her nametag read, 'Yawako Shimagawa.'

Yawako dashed across the room in her stocking feet. The tallest of the intruders saw her out of the corner of his eye and opened fire. She shrieked and covered her head as the poorly aimed shots sparked on the chrome wall above her. She skidded into the desk and stretched over the top of it. Making no attempt to take cover, she fumbled open one of the control panels and mashed the bright red emergency alarm button.

A round struck Yawako's extended arm. She screamed, but turned to face the attackers. She planned her feet at shoulder width, just as she had been taught in security training, and drew her sidearm awkwardly with her left hand. Tears streamed down her face like the blood running down her limp arm.

"Nobody move!" Her voice cracked, "Backup's on the way. Now drop your guns, and… and lie on the floor."

The woman in black waved off the gunman as he prepared to finish off Yawako.

"Vickie, a sec guard is a sec guard. Even if she's cute." He didn't speak, but rather sent the message through the wireless modem implanted at the base of his brain.

"I'll deal with her." Vickie responded over the airwaves.

"What are you? Lesbian?"

Vickie glared up at the hulking figure, wilting him. He lowered his head and turned back to the armored door. Another member of the team was busy connecting wires between his robotic forearm and the keypad built into the doorframe.

Vickie strode towards Yawako with the ominous clicking of high-heels on the marble floor. Her hair bounced around her like a model on the catwalk.

"St-st-stop or I'll…"

"Shoot!" Vickie taunted, as she walked into the barrel of the gun, pressing her chest against the end. She was a full head taller than Yawako.

Yawako shook so badly, she almost pulled the trigger by accident. Vickie's right hand snatched the gun away from Yawako.

Meanwhile, the left arm extended and snapped in, slapping Yawako across the face hard enough to turn her sideways. Vickie grabbed the front of the security uniform and lifted the stunned form off the ground. She gave a cruel smile and threw the petite guard to the floor, forcing her body though one of the wood and upholstery benches on the way down.

Yawako lay panting amid the splintered wreckage. The assault had ripped off the front of her shirt, exposing her bra which had a small superfluous pink bow in the middle.

"Aw, no flak vest." Vickie said in mock sympathy. She bent over and pressed Yawako's own gun against the bare skin over her heart.

"Cyan! Save me!" Yawako screamed before she was silenced by two loud bangs.

Moments earlier, Cyan Miller had stumbled down the stairs of a cargo plane. He didn't know if the blood on his green and tan uniform was his own or someone else's. He didn't really care at this point, but since most of the members of his team had more cyberware than flesh in their bodies, it was probably his.

Cyan was a cyborg, but he lacked the shining metal arms, super strength and bullet proof skin of his compatriots. The cyberneticians referred to Cyan as a "head case." The doctors had wired experimental computers into his brain and infusing the gray matter with nanites. One of the unexpected 'benefits' was the ability to remember everything. Or more precisely, the inability to forget anything, including the ordeal he'd just been through.

It had been a simple mission. One of CRI's sister companies, Bio Living Inc. sends collection teams around the word to bring back samples of exotic species. Money doesn't grow on trees, but miracle drugs do. Bio Living was looking for them in the heart of the Amazon rainforest: not a region known for its political stability. Intelligence reports had indicated the possibility of a renewed revolutionary offensive, so Bio Living had requested some of CRI's 'elite security personnel' to bring back their scientist.

Elite Security in this case meant five top-of-the-line paramilitary cyborgs with strength enhancers, reflex boosters, and infrared vision. Cyan had gone because he could establish a satellite-link and GPS signal anywhere in the world. He could also act as a central router, allowing the other team members to communicate not only thoughts, but what they were seeing or hearing as well.

The insertion went fine, but a 12 hour trek to the campsite through the summer rainforest is at best unpleasant. The biologists hadn't made camp where they had said they would. Dense foliage and the deepening night reduced Cyan's unaided visibility to nothing. It took the rest of the night to find the research team.

Physically, Cyan was the weak link in the cyborg team, but the scientists lagged even behind him. It took two days to the helicopter landing field. Meanwhile, the radio and satellite transmissions ringing in his head described the rapidly deteriorating political situation. He was able to hide the danger from the others, until they saw a shoulder-mounted missile rip out of the rainforest canopy and blow up their ride home.

The walk back to friendly territory was arduous. The others would never be able to forget it. Cyan would never be able to forget any of the details. The final tally was one scientist and one cyborg killed in a firefight, and one scientist dead from a combination of fever, dysentery, and dehydration. Another Bio Living employee had broken his femur, and the wound had subsequently become infected. He was still in a South American hospital, and would probably need to have his leg replaced with a cybernetic one.

"Yo, Twitch. We're going to go enjoy the alcoholic comforts of modern civilization." The words snapped Cyan back to the present. "You coming?"

"Bruce, will you stop calling me 'Twitch?'" Cyan turned to face the ranking member of the extraction team. Bruce was a large black male with a with silver arms, and a friendly face.

Bruce glanced down at Cyan's hands and smirked. Cyan looked down; his fingers were wiggling as if working on a phantom keyboard. He put his hands in his pockets and his nervous energy shifted to toe-tapping, "Sir, you know I'm not made of as tough of stuff as your men. I just want to get back to the Core and sleep it off."

"But we're going to catch it from Upstairs if you check in a couple of hours ahead of us."

"The corporate echelon doesn't care about you and your men having a little fun. They'll send down a disapproving memo, and then forget about it. In fact, they've probably already sent it since we're two days overdue." Reflexively, Cyan's mind reached out through the cellphone towers to CRI's central computer. He was just checking the backlog of messages when the lobby alarm went off. His eyes unfocused as he viewed the world through the security camera in reception area.

"What... Yawako, get out of there!" Cyan yelled and lunged forward.

"Hey Twitch, you okay?" Bruce's artificial hands grabbed his shoulders, firmly but gently.

"Bruce, get your men in the van." Cyan thought to him over their computer connection, "Weapons and live ammo! We have to go crash a little party at the Core."

The command spread at the speed of thought. One man passed out the M60 machineguns while the others piled in the back of the unmarked white van which had been waiting for them. Cyan took the driver's seat. He didn't even see the security booth as he drove through the lowered toll-arm. All he could see was Yawako lying in a growing pool of her own blood.

"What did I tell you?" Vickie smiled over her shoulder as she jogged towards the main entrance. "Piece of cake."

She looked forward again and was blinded by oncoming headlights. Her eyes' flare compensation program kicked in just in time for her to see the white van jump curb and slam airborne into the front glass wall. The wall was bulletproof, but the speeding van broke through in a burst of shards.

Vickie shielded her face with the right hand and reflexively struck back. Her left fist punched through the grillwork and radiator before the cooling fan sliced off her fingers and wrist. She slammed against the front of the van like an insect, and was carried through the security desk and into the far wall.

Cyan could barely see through his tears. Yawako's murderess was pinned to the wall by the van. She hung motionless; impaled on the debris of the desk. Behind him, he heard the panel door slide open, and three machineguns opened fire in unison. From the shotgun seat, Bruce fired his personalized semiautomatic, sawed-off shotgun.

Rather than watch the ensuing carnage, Cyan leapt out of the driver's seat and knelt down next to Yawako. He cradled her head against his chest and rocked back and forth.

"Hey, Twitch, you all right?"

After a long pause, Bruce crawled out over the bucket seats, "Well, there's not much left of those guys, but we can probably find an intact head if you want to try a little post-mortem interrogation. They say brain damage doesn't set in for five minutes."

Five minutes... The time stamp from the security camera flashed in front of Cyan's eyes. Yawako had been dead less than four minutes. He scooped her limp form over his shoulder and sprinted around the van. The door to the Core hung open from having been forced. The elevator was already on the lobby floor, having been used to bring the intruders back up, but the trip down to the B1 surgery level took seconds that Cyan couldn't spare.

Bursting into the first occupied surgery, he dropped Yawako quickly but lovingly onto the table. He stood coated in blood, quivering, and drew his gun on the cyberdoctors of his own company, "Save her... save her now!"

"Man! Now, you really look like you need a drink," Bruce's words pulled Cyan back from the brink of sleep. "Why don't you go lie down?"

"Can't... I have to be here when she comes out."

"What's your connection to that flesh-and-blood chick anyways, Twitch?" Bruce sat down next to him in the waiting room.

"Will you stop calling me..." Cyan realized that he was holding a magazine upside down and flipping the pages backwards. He cleared his throat, "We're dating. In the high-school sense of the word. Nothing physical. When the other guards would barely look up from their coffee cups, she would demand to see my credentials, and she looked them over so seriously. I appreciate her dedication, and the way she looks in that uniform. She... she's always so scared, but she seems to think I'm safe."

"Safe?" the commando laughed, "I guess she hasn't seen your driving?"

Cyan winced, "I'm just thankful the suits paid top dollar to put the Core near the airport."

"That reminds me. They called some suit away from a black tie dinner to explain your little stunt to the cops. If anyone asks, that van was stolen and used as part of the break in." Bruce motioned past the glass partition to the next room, where an anglo male with golden blonde hair was talking with a masked doctor, "That's the guy over there. Recognize him?"

Cyan had never seen the man before, but it only took 1.4 seconds to pull his profile from the company archives. Cyan began mumbling as he wirelessly downloaded the file. "Fredrick Temple. Age 38. Years with company: 16. Current Capacity: Junior Vice President in charge of CRI's in house R&D department. Previous Capacities... this guy changes jobs like you change gun clips."

"Incompetent?"

"More like extremely competent and extremely political."

The doctor finished speaking to Mr. Temple and moved into the room where Cyan and Bruce were seated, "The surgery was successful, the patient should be reviving soon if you want..."

Cyan left the doctor mid-sentence and entered the surgery. His heart caught in his throat. Yawako lay in a pool of blood on one of the surgical tables. She stared at him with unseeing eyes which were lit from behind by the light coming through her open skull cap. He forced himself to look away. On one of the other tables was an anglo-women with perfect proportions, a beautiful face and long blonde hair. Leaning against the walls in coffin-like boxes were three more identical women; three more units of the same model cyborg-body.

The supermodel cyborg on the operating table stirred. Cyan rushed to her side, "Yawako."

"Cyan...? You're late." It had a hint of her uncertainty, but it was not Yawako's voice, "You promised to take me to the ice cream shop."

"That was when I thought I'd be back around noon on Monday. You mean you haven't left the building in three days?"

Yawako nodded; her new artificial muscles snapping her head forward and backwards like a rag doll. After settling she continued speaking, "When you weren't back at closing time on Monday, I waited a couple minutes for you, then a couple more. Before I knew it, it had been hours and there was still no word from you. Some of the cybernetic soldiers in the Core promised to tell me if they heard anything, so I waited. And then it was morning and I had to go back to work. It seemed silly to leave when you must be so close. And so..."

"Well, lets go get you some ice cream."

"I don't want any ice cream!" The edge on her voice froze Cyan. Yawako had never spoken to him like that.

She smiled, "You're tired, and I don't know how to move yet. Let's save the ice cream for when we can enjoy it."

"If that's what you want," Cyan said cautiously. "I'll come find you as soon as I wake up and show you around the Core."

As he left, Cyan bumped into a table and Yawako's real body, the one he recognized, tumbled into his arms.

"Let's be honest," the graying psychiatrist regarded Cyan pacing in front of his large oak desk. "This has nothing to do with Yawako. You've objected to that body ever since you had the doctors put her brain in it at gunpoint."

"This *is* about Yawako." Cyan ran both hands through his short hair, still pacing, "She doesn't recognize herself in the mirror. She keeps destroying small objects by accident, and I've heard from her roommate that she doesn't so much as flinch in her sleep."

Dr. Hynes took an exasperated breath, "Full body cyborgs don't move in their sleep. It's a safety precaution against violent sleep walking."

"You're lying. I've heard the cyber docs talking. No one has a clue why some full body cyborgs sleep like the dead, but they're sure it's not a good sign. Look, I know it's not a cure-all, but what would it hurt to resculpt her face into a more natural one."

"You mean one more to your taste," Dr. Hynes went on the offensive. "You want everything to be like it was before the attack."

"Yes! Well close to that."

"I think you have rose-colored memories."

"Doc, I remember perfectly, too perfectly... the answer to question 37 on the first memory test you gave me is still 'c.'"

"I don't question your recollection of the facts; it's your interpretation of them. Yawako was physically weak. That resulted in an inferiority complex and dependency. You filled that dependency. Now we have corrected the root of the complex," he gave a cruel smile, "and she doesn't need you anymore."

Cyan stormed out of the office slamming the door. At the first cross hall he turned the corner and collided with a female cyber soldier. The impact knocked him to the floor, but left her unfazed.

"Watch where you're going!" She snapped.

"Nice to see you too, Yawako." He hadn't recognized her at first.

"Oh, Cyan. I'm sorry. Are you alright?" She knelt down besides him.

"I'm fine. But I think Dr. Hynes needs to get his head examined."

"Really? What did he say to you?"

"He said... it was nothing." Cyan got back to his feet.

"Dr. Hynes has come up with a way to help me with the anger over my..." Yawako hesitated, "death. We've tracked down the company those infiltrators were from. The doc got me assigned to a retribution strike."

Cyan froze. His mind raced too fast for his mouth to explain his thoughts. Instinctively he reached out to her through the airwaves, "The good doctor prescribed revenge? That goes against everything he's been taught. I don't know what they've been doing to you or what they have planned, but there is more to this. The company uses all of us like property, you're no exception. Be careful. You can't just trust in—"

"I'm not a little girl!" Yawako screamed verbally, "Don't tell me what to do!"

Cyan backed against the wall and slumped shoulders, "You're right. Regardless of how you feel about me, I don't want you to come to harm. I'd like to go on that strike mission with you."

"I'm taking Bruce. It's reassuring to have a big, dumb tough who's good with a shotgun."

Again Cyan's mind extended into the wireless regime. This time it was not a general broadcast, but a private line, "Bruce, I have a favor to ask."

Bruce Washington sat back from the cafeteria table and folded his arms across his chest. He regarded Yawako dispassionately for a moment, "You may have them running scared in the training dojo, but you have a lot to learn about strategy. I am trained and augmented for paramilitary situations. Unless you plan on starting a war with Technology Life, I won't be much good to you."

"You trained in stealth."

"Warzone stealth. What you're doing is completely different.

Given some foliage cover, I could get near the building without being seen. With all the cameras and open ground, you *will* be seen. What you have to do is not get *noticed*."

"What do you suggest?" Yawako looked down, embarrassed by being lectured in public.

"I was just getting to that. With all the computerized security in research facilities, you need a head case with you. Lucas Wilko is the latest model, but new isn't always improved, if you follow me. Now, I worked with Cyan Miller during that rainforest debacle. Twitch is good at his job and has the grit for bearing adversity I wish all of my combat models had."

"But Cyan is a lousy shot and his hand-to-hand skills are even worse."

"You should see the damage he can do with a van."

Yawako went rigid, "Fine. I'll go ask Cyan if he still wants to come."

From his room down the hall, Cyan had been eavesdropping on Bruce through his wireless brain connection. "Thanks, Bruce. I owe you."

"That wasn't for you. That is my honest tactical assessment of the situation. Now you're responsible for keeping that little spitfire out of trouble."

Cyan had to admit that the reception of Technology Life's research facility was more impressive than CRI's. The high ceiling was supported by columns of white marble. The lighting wasn't glaring, but left no shadows. The room was expansive, made to seem even more so by the mirrors covering the walls which made it difficult to tell where the real rows of columns ended and the reflections started. Beneath the transparent floor, the pillars were tapered to make it seem like much more than the actual meter it was down to the screens displaying an overhead view of slowly moving clouds.

Cyan must have been staring, because Yawako thought to him, "It is an artistic interpretation of living inside a computer."

The thought took Cyan aback. All of the times he'd accessed various systems, he'd never thought about what it was like "inside a computer." But this wasn't it. If he had to put it into a metaphor, it would be more like crawling around black tunnels with the only source of light being red stock tickers of data streaming along every surface in every direction.

Then a second thought took Cyan aback, "That wasn't in our briefing."

"I did some research of my own." Yawako replied, then went on to quote what had been in the briefing, "Their building is arranged like ours. The research surgeries and barracks are located in subterranean levels. The only access point is a secure elevator off the main lobby."

"What about fire escape stairs?"

"You're assuming the company cares if we die."

They had perfect confidence speaking candidly back and forth over their wireless link. No one would ever suspect two janitors of having the hardware needed for such a conversation. And thanks to power management, someone would have to be within about a meter to pick up the broadcasts. Even then, the average time to break one of CRI's encryption programs was three months.

Getting this far had been easy. Technology life didn't hire very security-conscious cleaning crews. One of CRI's other agents had lifted the security RFID tags off a couple of the day crew by posing as another employee sneaking out for an unscheduled smoke break. Between those and the easily counterfeited uniforms, none of the outer perimeter check points had thought to check the janitors' cart. But getting into the research facility itself would be the hard part.

"You go for the door. I'll neutralize the guards."

Cyan nonchalantly drifted to the right as Yawako approached the security desk. According to the report, Technology Life used implanted radio ID chips in its security cyborgs rather than a number code like CRI. In theory that was more secure because it would take surgery to steal one of the encoded chips, but Cyan was confident he could crash the lock system once it opened a channel with him.

Yawako turned the cart sideways in front of the guards, "Could ya hand me the trash can?"

"Oh, right." The guard on the left make no attempt to hide his annoyance. He slid his chair back and leaned under the desk. Yawako snatched a 30 cm blade from its hiding point on the cart and vaulted over the counter. She drove the blade into the base of the other security guard's throat at a steep angle. It entered above the flack jacket, piercing down through the esophagus, lungs, heart and maybe even lower organs. Death was assured, but not instant.

The remaining guard jumped, banging his head on the counter. He slid back just in time for Yawako to bring an axe kick down on the back of his head. The force of the blow flipped him out of the chair. He rolled over onto his back, still trying to figure out what was happening. Yawako smashed her heel down on his throat, crushing the trachea. Again, death was assured, but not instant.

Cyan stared at Yawako in shock. Fortunately, his subconscious never stopped working on the security lock, and it popped open with a distressed beep.

"What are you waiting for? Call the elevator! I'll grab the hardware!" Yawako said as she shoved the head of the first guard backwards and withdrew her knife. Blood bubbled up out of the small incision like water from a fountainhead.

As the elevator arrived, Yawako trotted up with a satchel slung over her left shoulder and the knife in her right hand. She also had a .45 from one of the guards tucked into her belt. "Between how quietly those two went down and your slick work on that lock, they haven't sounded an alarm yet, but that doesn't mean we should waste time."

Cyan nodded, trying to focus on the mission and not the trail of blood drops the knife was leaving. "According to the electric meter records, the mainframes are probably on the 4th floor."

Cyan pressed the B4 button in the elevator. Nothing happened. He pushed it again, this time holding it down. Nothing happened.

Yawako switched the knife to her left hand, reached over, held down the "Door Close" button with her thumb, and pressed B4 with her pointer finger. The button lit up and the elevator started to move.

"How did you know to do that?"

"It's a standard security procedure."

Now that she mentioned it, Cyan had heard of this kind of safeguard, but that training had been before his memory upgrade, so he didn't have instant command of it.

The elevator reached the 4th basement with a "ding." The basement floor was also painted white. Rather than the heavenly motif of the lobby, it was an antiseptic hospital white. Yawako strode forwards, passed two doors, stopped at a third, and punched in the access code. The light on the door lock turned green.

Cyan reached into the janitor's overalls and drew the small 9mm he was carrying. He pointed at the woman in front of him, "Who are you and how did you know the correct room and the combination?"

She looked at him stunned and said in a trembling voice, "Cyan, it's me."

For an instant Cyan believed her. Then Yawako screamed and threw her head back. She dropped the knife and grabbed her head staggering around the hallway. Panting, she looked up at him and gave a cruel smile, "So you haven't perfected Suppressive Chip technology yet."

The next thing Cyan knew, he was doubled over on the ground. Even though he had had his gun trained on her, she had still been able to draw the .45 from her belt and shoot him through the chest before he could react.

The woman stood over Cyan laughing. "This is what they sent me to CRI to steal. So nice of you to give us a free sample."

Now Cyan recognized her. The face was different but the expression was the same as when she had killed Yawako.

Vickie kicked Cyan's gun away from him, and leaned down to gloat over him, "We might have to try one of these things on you. You see, the problem with captives is even if you make them tell you 'everything' they still leave things out. Like that elevator trick. What a Suppressive Chip is supposed to do is subvert the original personality with more loyal one, while still retaining all of the memories. Unfortunately, to copy an entire personality you have to stick so many probes into the brain that you destroy it. Wasn't CRI lucky to have that pathetic little bitch 'volunteer' her brain."

"Don't you dare talk about Yawako like that!"

"No, Cyan, it's okay. She's right. I've always been weak," The woman looked as surprised at her own words as Cyan. "I thought becoming a security officer would make me strong, but I didn't understand. Strength comes from having something to protect. I know I'm weak, but now I can be as strong as I have to be to save you."

With a trembling hand the woman started to raise the gun towards her own temple. Her expression flashed between paralyzing panic and calm resolve.

Cyan knew his body wouldn't be fast enough, so he reached out with his mind. Not just contacting her like before, but entering into her mind the way he would a computer system. If a computer system was like crawling around dark tunnels, this was like getting thrown around in a black storm cloud, with only blinding flashes of lightning to see by. Cyan searched frantically, not knowing what he was looking for or where he was going. Then everything went calm and bright, as if he had broken out of the clouds into clear air above.

Physically, Yawako gave Cyan a sad smile and pulled the trigger.

Cyan never heard the gunshot. Thanks to his mental connection he convulsed as if it was his own brain now plastered on the wall. When he finally came to, the time stamp showed that he had been unconscious for two minutes.

Someone had probably heard the gunshots and sounded the alarm. Cyan started to crawl back towards the elevator.

"Yo, Twitch. You hear the good news? Somebody's hydroelectric plant is about to flood some ruins in India, so we get to go blow up the dam."

"Since when does the company care about cultural treasures?" Cyan sat down on the locker room bench gingerly. It had been a month, but the bullet wound in his chest still hurt if he moved the wrong way.

"It doesn't. But how often do you get a chance to trash somebody's billion dollar project and blame it on religious radicals."

A trip to India? Cyan could just hear Yawako, "Would you please take me to see the ruins?"

Cyan froze. He really could hear Yawako's voice! He spun around. The chest wound stung, but he barely noticed. Yawako was standing there behind him. It was not the artificial body, but her real form: a small Asian woman with short hair and thick, wire rim glasses. Her green and tan uniform was impeccably clean and pressed. Before he could ask even one of the hundreds of questions flooding his mind she put a finger over his lips.

"Don't talk to me because I'm not really here." To emphasis the point, her form went translucent for a moment. "I'm just an illusion dancing in front of your eyes. Just think. I can hear your thoughts."

"...How?"

"Well, Dr. Hynes would say that the stress of your augmentations, and having to watch your girlfriend die twice has driven you to schizophrenia. And thanks to the information you pulled from the Suppressive Chip you have created a surprisingly accurate hallucination."

"And what would what would Yawako Shimagawa say?"

"Do you remember when you connected to me just before... well... just before I saved you? You went much deeper than my mind. You reached the soul trapped on that little chip. And you refused to let go, even when... well." She shifted uncomfortably. "But anyways, thanks your computer implants there is more than enough room for both of us in your skull. So now I'm your personal binary angel."

"I don't have a physical body, it just feels like something is touching you." She tapped her finger on his lips, "So you'll have to yield to any pressure I apply, or you'll go right through me."

"What are you talking about?"

Rather than answering in words, Yawako bent over and kissed him. It might not have been real, but her lips were soft and warm against his. He could even feel the breath from her nose tickling his cheek.

A chorus of wolf whistles and cat calls filled the locker room.

Yawako jumped and looked around, "What's happening?"

After a moment of consideration, Cyan rubbed the base of his skull where the wireless modem was implanted and spoke verbally this time, "I must be subconsciously transmitting your image and voice to everyone who would be able to see you if you were here."

The door burst open. Dr. Hynes stood in the doorway and scanned the room, looking straight through Yawako. Not finding her, he glared at Cyan.

Cyan smiled up at Yawako, "Everyone on our wireless grid can see you, including the security cameras."

Yawako's face flushed bright red as she turned to face the rest of the locker room. She closed her eyes and gave a weak wave,

RAMSEY LUNDOCK

"Hi, everyone! I'm back!"

Dead Zone

"No Signal."

The message from his implanted modem flashed though Loki's brain. He would have crashed the car out of shock if he hadn't been driving ponderously to navigate the pothole-pocked dirt track winding though the forest.

Mentally he tried boosting his own signal strength only to find that it was already at maximum. That at least explained why he had a splitting headache. The only time he had ever lost signal before was in a bank vault. Fortunately, that robbery had been over in a matter of minutes.

Loki divided his attention between steering around the puddles of unknown depth dotting the road and running a diagnostic check on his modem. Had his receiver gone dead? No, he could still contact his car's wireless systems. Somebody must be jamming the airwaves. But there was no flood of white noise; there was simply "No Signal." He had heard that away from the cities there were still dead zones where you couldn't connect to the grid, but Loki had assumed those were places like Antarctica and the Himalayans. He hadn't expected to find one south of Jacksonville.

Loki looked for a place to pull over and collect his thoughts, but oak trees stood in thick underbrush right next to the path. Branches from those giant trees stretched overhead, filtering out the scorching noon day sun.

Loki still had the driving directions he had been given, which said to stay on this road, if you could call it that. This street wasn't on any of the maps. He had had a devil of a time finding it after he pulled off of the freeway. He never would have recognized it as a road if not for the patches of asphalt showing through the thick layer of grass. But the pavement and grass had both ended several miles back.

He called up the satellite map which he had downloaded before heading out and cross referenced against the GPS coordinates the car's navi-computer was feeding him. There had to be some mistake. Even at the highest resolution, there was no trail in the picture. Some hacker must be feeding him false GPS coordinates. He couldn't possibly have driven into the middle of that unbroken stretch of forest canopy. Could he?

Almost afraid of what he might see, Loki leaned forward and looked up though the windshield. He couldn't see the sky. All he could see was a roof of branches with white tangles of some kind of moss hanging from them. This was a tunnel under the oak canopy, hidden from satellite cameras.

The sweat running down his face wasn't just from the heat. He took a deep breath. For the first time since he had gotten his wireless implants, which was longer ago than he could remember, Loki was lost. At least until there was a fork in the road, he only had one option: forward.

The scenery didn't change for what seemed like an eternity. Actually it was 47 minutes and 32 seconds, according to his neural implant computer's clock, before Loki spotted a white single-story building through the trees ahead on the right. Cross referencing the satellite photo with his GPS feed, he could see there was a small white clearing up ahead. A little closer and his physical eyes could see a large yellow sign out front.

"PORK CHOPS 12S"

On the far side of the building Loki could see a variety of vehicles parked on a field of limestone gravel next to the building. The limestone must be what he was seeing on the satellite view.

He could reconnect to the grid via one of the restaurant's terminals, even if he had to hack it.

Loki pulled into the parking lot and slammed on the brakes. He couldn't believe his eyes. There, tied to a rail under the shade of a tree at the back of the parking lot, were two horses!

Loki preformed a mental log off, incase this was some virtual reality game he had gotten too engrossed in. But no, this was reality.

He couldn't sit there blocking the entrance, and besides, he was hungry. He pulled into what he assumed was a parking space between two cars; it didn't have an auto-docking signal to mark the boundaries. He got out, put his car's security system into semi-lethal mode and went into the building, glancing over his shoulder one more time. Yes, those were definitely horses.

Before he got all the way in the door, Loki could feel all the eyes in the restaurant focus on him. Not surprising, even in the sweltering heat, he hadn't thought it prudent to take off his armored jacket with the Tomb Rats' gang symbol painted across the back. He could see some of the other patrons were wearing boots, but they were cowboy boots, unlike his own over the knee biker-boots. But more than the clothes, they were staring at his metallic silver eyes and the block of six data terminals sitting between the temple and ear on the right side of his head.

He tried to pretend like he didn't notice, and took a seat with his back in the corner. Even inside, the restaurant was still a dead zone. He checked for a physical outlet where he could connect. If everyone was going to stare at his data terminals, he might as well use them. No outlets. How did people check the menu and place their orders? More importantly, how was he going to hack the grid to get directions?

Loki fought down the panic. He reminded himself that unlike grid-runners, he could solve problems without using computers. Sometimes you had to get physical.

Loki identified a small woman with a blonde ponytail as the waitress. Just before he shouted her down, he realized; she wasn't just delivering food, she was taking orders too. So that's how it worked. He just had to wait his turn.

After the waitress had taken orders from a couple who had come in after him, Loki started drumming his fingers on the table and repeatedly clearing his throat. He made it a point not to stay places where he wasn't welcome, but in this dead zone, he had no way of knowing where the next restaurant was.

At last, the waitress arrived. She wouldn't even look directly at him, but at least she asked, "Whaddya want to eat?"

How was he supposed to know that? He hadn't seen a menu. But Loki didn't want to push his already thin welcome too far. He didn't even know the name of this place. All the sign out front had said was...

"Pork chops!" Loki blurted out.

"And drink?"

"Whatever the local cola is." At least that answer was always the same.

It was another 20 minutes before the food arrived. They must really not like him to take that long to microwave it, but Loki wasn't going to bail out after getting his order placed.

Pork chops was an understatement. The plate arrived with two pork chops, mixed vegetables and a mound of mashed potatoes with brown gravy covering every square inch of the plate. Of course no matter what mold you pressed the nutrient mix into, it all tasted the same. The whole meal smelled like the aftermath of a napalm grenade.

Loki picked up the fork and tried to cut off the tip of the one of the pork chops. No luck, it was too tough. So he tried the mashed potatoes.

Whatever nutrient mix this place was using, Loki wanted a box of it to go. The gravy and the mashed potatoes were actually different flavors! He swirled them around in his mouth. With a taste like this, he could forgive them for the lumps. After all, no matter how well you mix the nutrient flakes, there are always a few lumps left. But when he bit these lumps, they weren't dry and powdery; they were chewy chunks.

As he shoveled the piping hot mashed potatoes into mouth, Loki noticed there had been a knife wrapped up in the napkin with the fork. That must be for the pork chops. He paused for breath and to let the hot mass of potatoes settle into his stomach, and used the time to grab the knife and slash one of the pork chops. The attack left only a slight groove in the top. He stabbed the thing with his fork and sawed back and forth with the knife.

No food was this tough to cut. Yet there was something familiar about the action: the repetitive sawing motion, following the grain of the flesh to make the cutting easier, the familiar scraping sound when the knife hit the bone. It reminded him of cutting the cyber-arm off of a downed chrome crazy to sell the 'used' cyberware to a black market street doc.

Loki stared in disbelief at the morsel on the end of his fork. Could it really be that this was real food? It smelled like a charred corpse; it cut like muscle. He was in a dead zone with horses out front: at this point anything was possible. No wonder they hadn't wanted to serve him. Loki didn't even want to think about how much credit this was going to set him back, but it was worth it.

Loki finished the meal by literally licking the plate clean and gnawing the bones until they snapped between his teeth. Now it wasn't his implants that people were staring at. But he didn't care. He was only going to get one chance to eat real food in his life, so he wasn't going to leave any behind. The cola, which was normally needed kill the taste of the nutrient mix, had barely been touched over the course of the meal.

He let out a contented sigh and walked to a machine by the door to the kitchen. Everyone else had stopped by the machine on their way out. That must be the credit terminal. The waitress broke off taking drinks to one of the other tables and maneuvered behind the machine.

"The special and a cola. That will be 14 Silvers. Plus, you forgot to leave a tip."

"Just let me connect to the grid and I'll remember to tip."

"Oh sure. I'm carrying a grid connection in my pocket."

Loki waited a couple of heartbeats for her to pull out the grid connection, then realized she had been being sarcastic. Meanwhile the waitress' humor went from foul to hostile.

"Frank, I think we got a deadbeat!" she called into the kitchen.

A mountain of a man in a white apron lumbered out of the back room carrying a meat cleaver longer than Loki's forearm. There was the same aura of napalm victim around him that had wafted from the pork chops. Loki considered going for the gun in his underarm holster, but since half the patrons were carrying pieces on their hips, he wouldn't win a shootout. Instead he raised his hands to shoulder level.

"Look, I got credit. Just let me connect to the grid and..."

"We don't take credit, certainly not from some chrome freak stranger. You'd better cough up the Silvers."

"I don't know what 'Silvers' are, but if you give me some time..."

Wrong thing to say. The hairy giant raised the meat cleaver over his head. Loki danced backwards, and grabbed for his pistol. The waitress beat him to the draw with a small revolver that must have been hidden behind the counter.

"Frank! Lucy! I'll pay his tab!"

That stopped them in their tracks. Loki slowly and carefully pulled his hand out of his jacket, showing his two assailants that it was still empty.

The voice had come from a man in a soiled white t-shirt, ripped jeans, and a worn green baseball cap, "I'm headed to the bank anyways."

His savior handed Lucy a fist full of paper. She inspected the papers and put them into the machine on the counter and started to hand him back some different pieces of paper.

He raised his hand refusing them. "Keep it. For the fuss."

Then he turned to Loki, "Come with me, boy. After you've traded credit for Silvers down at the bank, you can pay me back."

Loki followed him out and started moving towards his faded blue economy car, "I guess I'll follow you to the bank."

"Nuh uh," he shook his head. "You get in your car and take off? No! Ride with me." He jerked his thumb towards a pickup truck the same color as his hat.

Loki went around to the passenger door and waited to be let in. He mentally contacted his car and upgraded the security to "Lethal."

Neither one of them spoke again until the truck had pulled out of the parking lot.

"You saved me back there. I would have done some damage on the way down, but there was no way I was going to walk away from that one."

"Watching an idiot get killed while I'm eating spoils my appetite. You got a name, boy?"

"Loki."

"Loki? Why not?" He took his left hand off the steering wheel and reached across his body, "Chris Thompson."

Loki shook his hand, "Look, about the bank. I *will* pay you back, but I have to warn you my system identification number's been razed. If the bank tries to run a background check, we're both going to get arrested."

"Relax. I don't even have a SID number. No one out here does."

"That doesn't make any sense. Anyone who was born at a hospital has a SID number. Anyone who's ever been arrested or gone to school or received a gov welfare check has a SID."

"Like I said, no one out here has a SID. Heck, there are entire towns out here in the Forest that aren't on any maps."

"How is that possible?"

"Well, with all the required technology, some people couldn't afford to keep upgrading. Others just decided to opt out. Some folks around here believe a SID is the Mark of the Beast. About 50 years ago, the hippie tribe went downright technophobic and started blowing up wireless towers. They say they're a secret government plot to track people."

Actually, it was fairly simple using wireless towers to triangulate the position of an implanted modem, or even a handheld grid interface. But Loki decided it best not to point that out.

"Once folk figured out no SID meant no taxes, even the Sheriff and the county judges stopped registering. The city sprawls have always ignored the countryside. And we just don't draw attention to ourselves."

An entire dead zone civilization.

"But you've drawn a lot of attention to yourself. So unless you got a dern good reason, as soon as you pay me back, you'd better get back in your car and go back to where you came from."

"I'm out here to meet a client. Somebody by the handle Slim Jones asked me to meet him out here."

"Well then it's a good thing I'm taking you to the bank."

"Why's that?"

"Slim owns it."

The bank was a one-story brick building with faux Grecian columns out front. The security guard rested his hand on his revolver as Loki followed Chris through the iron barred front doors.

Loki scanned the room. The doors would be easy to force with a pry bar, two kg of plastic explosives would open the vault door. Actually, it looked like the vault wasn't quite shut as it was. The only thing to be careful about was the painting of a lighthouse, which hung so that it covered part of the metal frame surrounding the vault door. It must be concealing something; maybe a tear gas canister, or claymore mine, depending on if they wanted the intruders alive or dead. He estimated a half decent team could clean the place out in 15 minutes. But that wasn't why he was here.

Chris was talking to a woman behind a counter, a human ATM, "Yeah, I need to make a withdrawal, and 'Loki' here would like to buy some Silvers with credit."

The ATM's pensive look dissolved into a predatory smile, "We're always willing to buy credit. How much are you looking to sell?"

"How about 200 'Silvers' worth?"

"That will be 137 credit please. You can use the terminal over there to make the transfer." She indicated an archaic computer gathering dust in the corner.

Loki fished around in his pockets and found his cable. He connected one of the data ports on his head directly to the jack on the back of the computer box. Like always, Loki hacked the connection password to make the transaction harder to trace. He was shocked to discover that after defeating that token security barrier, he had access to the entire system. Wait, there was only a single account, with 16 credit in it. This must be only a subsystem. Loki made a quick scan, more out of habit than real curiosity. Unless the secret door to the rest of the system was better hidden than any he had ever seen, this really was the entire system.

The credit transfer system was painfully slow and Loki doubted that his direct interface saved him any time. At the same time, being able to reconnect to the grid, even if it was a noisy, slow, land-line connection without virtual reality capability, felt like filling his lungs with fresh air after being trapped underwater for the past several hours.

After finishing with Chris, the ATM walked out on to the floor and handed Loki a stack of blue printed papers, "Now if you need more, just come back any time we're open, and we'll be happy to get you some more Silvers."

She leaned closer and said in a stage whisper, "Actually, next time if I go back and talk to the Manager, I think I can get you a better exchange rate."

The numbers '20' were printed in each corner of the bill. In the center, under the intricate design depicting a bald eagle perching in an oak tree, the bill bore the words "Redeemable for 1.00 oz of silver at Green Oak Bank." He leafed through the stack and found the ATM had given him various denominations going down all the way down to 'Half.'

"I figure, including your part of the tip, you owe me about 18 of those."

Loki peeled out a 20 and a 5 and thrust them into Chris' calloused hand. Loki cut off his objections, "Keep it. For the fuss."

Then Loki turned to the ATM, "Now, where can I find Slim Jones?"

'Slim' Jones was anything but. Having long ago lost the Battle of the Bulge, his belt had called in suspenders for reinforcements to help keep his pants up. What little brown hair he had left clung precariously to the sides of his head like a rock climber.

"Please take a seat," he motioned to one of the blue leather chairs in front of his desk, then collapsed back into his own chair, which groaned under his weight.

This was the first time Loki had felt air conditioning since leaving his car.

Slim regarded Loki with open distaste and dissatisfaction, "So you're the city slicker operative they sent out?"

"My agent, Glamour, said you had specifically requested me."

"Well, yeah. You see, we ain't got much love for outsiders here in Green Oak..."

"I've noticed."

"But I've got a job that needs to be kept low key. And since that's your name, I thought you'd be a little more discrete."

Low key? Loki could barely stifle his laugh. He had been told that if he made it big, he'd score jobs on his name alone. But he hadn't expected them to come like this.

"Suzan told me you bought a stack of Silvers. Did you read some of them?"

Loki recovered his composure enough to nod.

"Back when the Fed switched from dollars to credit, my granddaddy realized there were folk out here who couldn't use credit. So he made a gamble and used all of his money and all the money in the bank to buy a truckload of silver. Then he started printing Silvers. And the gamble paid off. Some of the other banks printed their own money, but people stopped using them. Today Green Oak is the only bank in the Forest, because folks know that any time they want, they can trade in their bank notes for cold, hard metal."

An awkward pause followed. Slim glanced around the room, as if looking for something, "Well, there's no sense beating around the bush. We got robbed. Tuesday night, someone came in here, shot the night guard, Jimmy, and cleaned us out. This entire town is going to go ape if they find out their Silvers are worthless. So what I'm hiring you to do is investigate and get the silver back, without letting anyone know it's missing."

"And my fee?"

"I believe a 10 percent finder's fee is standard."

"Give me one good reason why I shouldn't just hunt down the silver and keep it for myself?"

"Well, I'm playing poker with Sheriff Hunt tonight. He likes city folk even less than most of us. I can either tell him that you're working for me, or I can tell him you came into my office and threatened me."

"All right, 10 percent. But I'm going to need 500 Silvers up front to cover operating costs."

Slim nodded his double chin.

Loki stood up and reached across the desk to shake his fat bloated hand, resisting the urge to wipe his own hand on his jeans afterwards. In the world of operatives, where a contract would be incriminating evidence, a handshake was binding.

"When you're asking questions, you can tell folk I hired you to track down Jimmy Morgan's killer, which isn't even a lie. But I've told 'em the vault door stopped the robbers. We've been keepin' the vault closed so no one can see it's empty."

"I guess the place to start is to watch the security camera footage."

"Oh, that thing hasn't worked in decades. We just leave it up there to discourage thieves."

"Very effective isn't it?" Loki continued before Slim could rebut him, "The front door wasn't forced, and the vault wasn't blown. Although those old fashioned dial locks are simple to pick if you've got any kind of built in hearing augmentation, it's even easier if you know the combination. I'm thinking inside job."

"The vault was forced with some kind of jaws-of-life. Broke the deadbolts clean off. I can show you the scratch marks if you want."

"They're under the painting of the lighthouse."

"Well, yeah. I was hoping no one would notice we had moved that. As for the front door, you got me. Maybe they told Jimmy they needed to use the bathroom or something. Jimmy was a good, honest man, but not real bright."

On his way out, Loki looked around. The town of Green Oak, if you could call it a town, was a single four-way stop intersection. The bank sat on the southwest corner. Catty-corner from the bank was a gas station. The northwest was a brown wooden building. The yellow paint was peeling off of the two-foot-tall plywood letters nailed above the door which read, "G OCERY". The southeast was a row of three conjoined storefronts, the same color as the grocery store; all of them abandoned.

Only the gas station and the bank had asphalt parking lots.

Loki could see fresh peel-out tire marks leading away from the parking space in front of the entrance of the bank, probably from the getaway vehicle. Following the trajectory with his eyes, he spotted where not two, but four strips had been ripped up on the grass median in front of the bank. Apparently the robbers hadn't bothered using the exit, which opened on the east side. That told him there were at least two vehicles and they had headed off to the west.

He also noticed a familiar green pickup truck with a pair of booted feet sticking out the driver's window.

"Chris, are you all right?"

Chris sat up and pulled the baseball cap off of his face, and wasted no time in returning it to his head, "Yeah. I just got to thinking, you'd probably need a ride back to your car, and it's on my way home."

"I can just get a taxi."

"Not in this town you can't."

As the truck pulled out, Chris looked around as if honestly expecting eavesdroppers, "I didn't want to say anything in front of Suzan, but you got screwed. One credit is worth at least two Silvers. Probably more right now, since the Import Store is out of credit."

"What's the Import Store?"

"You see, we're pretty self-reliant out here. But some things like refrigerators and car parts we have to buy from outside. That's what the Import Store is for, it has a credit account to bring stuff from outside, then we pay in Silvers. You can even order stuff, if it's not too hard to get ahold of, and the store has credit. But right now, all the credit's been spent, so no one can order anything until after next week's big watermelon market. At least until you made your transaction. In fact, I wouldn't be surprised if the reason you got such a bad exchange rate was because Suzan wants to order something costing 130 credit."

"You raise watermelons? Those things are worth 100 credit apiece."

"That's what I've been told. Of course that's after they've been shipped, refrigerated, injected with preservatives, artificial colors, and ripeners. Out here, at the height of the season, you have a hard time trading one for a gallon of gas. I take my crops to market; melons, beans, or peanuts depending on the season; and the corp buyers pay whatever they feel like. Its not a lot, but it pays the mortgage."

"How does the Import Store get the credit in the first place?"

"The corp. buyers pay credit for the crops. It all goes in a shell account down at the bank. They do the conversion to Silvers and pay us."

"And then you trade the Silvers for metallic silver."

"Na. I mean I could. I feel like it sometimes, but just I'd have to sell it back to the bank when I wanted to spend it, and they'd cheat me on the exchange rate again. The only thing I trade Silvers for is some credit at the Import Store around Christmas."

"But how does the Import Store get the credit from the shell account?"

"Yeah, you see, Slim owns the Import Store."

Loki pulled up in front of a weather-beaten, white cinderblock, art-deco building. Even badly faded, the green and pink color scheme managed to be nauseating. The peeling sign read "Island Motel." Without having to be told, he knew this was the only hotel in town.

He killed the engine and went in to the reception office. The shag carpet had been worn down to the cement slab floor in front of the desk. The receptionist's face was painted thick with makeup in a failed attempt to make her look half her age. The neckline cut down to navel was meant attract stares, but it make Loki want to look away, afraid of what he might see.

"We don't have any Silvers." The woman raised her hands when she saw Loki.

"Then I'll take a room instead." He had intended to pay, but why if he didn't have to? "And do you have some place I can access a map?"

"I can draw you a map back to the highway if you'd like."

"I'm not looking for the highway. I'm going to be staying here a while. I'll need to know my way around. I'll take the access code to the room now, and the map in the morning."

The receptionist blanched white under her base as she handed him an actual physical key, "You're going to be staying for a while?"

Loki moved his economy car to the space in front of the room, and turned on the car's radar, microphones, and IR cameras.

All the sensors drained the battery and killed the gas mileage, but it beat getting ambushed.

The motel room was dark except for the light leaking in around the curtains. It was just enough to interfere with his low-light vision enhancements but not enough to see by. Feeling along the walls, he found the light switch. He wished he hadn't found it. The decor was clashing mix of red and pink hearts and tropical island motifs. On the plus side, it was more spacious than the dives he was used to holing up in.

Loki dead-bolted the door and attached the chain. Then jammed one of the crumbling white wicker chairs under the doorknob for what good it would do. He gave the room quick a paranoia security check. Satisfied, he placed his gun on the nightstand where it would be more accessible, and let his body drop onto the perfumed sheets. He drifted off to sleep to the sound of the dripping bathroom faucet and the whir of the window-mounted AC unit.

Loki was awakened in the predawn hours by his car's security sensors. Radar, thermalgraphic, and microphones all agreed: someone was tiptoeing up to his door. Only one person, a woman from that thermal silhouette. Loki opted for first strike instead of holing up. He grabbed his gun, kicked the wicker chair away from the door and undid the latches. He waited until the intruder was right in front of the door. Like he expected, she didn't try to knock, instead kneeling down. Loki flung open the door and pointed his gun point blank at her forehead.

The receptionist screamed.

"Do you usually sneak around your own motel?"

"I... I... I was only going to slip the map under your door."

Loki holstered his 9mm, took the hand-drawn map and started cross correlating it against his satellite images. He could tell she had a lousy sense of direction and a worse sense of distance. But if he looked at the map as a schematic, it gave him some idea what turns to make and what the roofs he could see poking out of the canopy were. The intersection which made up the town of Green Oak was near the west edge of the map."

"Hey, what's... You can stand up. I'm not going to shoot you. What's out there past the bank?"

"Oh, I don't think you want to go down there. That's the

black neighborhood."

There were five other patrons in the bar when Loki walked in from the hot muggy afternoon. At least two of them were underage. They all had piecemeal cybernetic implants: an arm here, a pair of eyes there. He didn't see any data terminals, and no one was broadcasting wirelessly. One guy was wearing shorts to show off his gleaming gold cybernetic leg. Augmented legs only did you any good if you had two of them, and ruling out the possibility the guy was an honest accident victim; the cyberware had been chosen for its brand name and not its effectiveness. The all wore the same gang colors: red and gold.

Even though Tomb Rat colors were black and yellow, Loki would have fit right in if not for the color of his skin.

"You lookin' for trouble, mister?"

"Not looking for trouble; running from it. Even I wouldn't think of looking for myself in here."

The guy with the golden leg laughed, "Dat sho is true."

The others relaxed and smiled.

"It's hot. I need a cold beer. You guys want one?"

Loki had intended to lose a couple games of pool to put a little money in circulation. But these guys were good enough, he found he could play as well as he could, in full confidence of losing.

Willie, the bartender, took the bowl of shells from the edge of the pool table and replaced it with a fresh empty bowl, "Da way you eating dese things, I should be chargin' you for da boiled peanuts an givin' you da beer fo' free."

Loki couldn't answer because he was in the midst of slurping the salty mixture out of the shell to keep it from running down his chin as he sucked the soft peanuts into his mouth, "These things are addictive."

"Don' say at too loud. King Death's boys'll be sellin' 'em on da corner."

"Man, we do sell 'em! Least when Bubba Hunt's watchin'."

"No wonder you guys can afford the expensive chrome. Where I come from, drugs are good money. Of course, in the city no one can grow anything, so they have to bring it all in." Loki hoped they couldn't tell he was lying. Street dealers were never any better off than the population they were fleecing. And as far as 'expensive' chrome; the wiring in his head was worth more than the rest of them combined. Of course pointing that out would be a good way to get his head cut off.

"We don' grow nuthin' neither. 'Cept the weed." Jamal, the one with the golden leg laughed, "An da peanuts. King Death knows some guys who bring da junk up from South America."

At last, the conversation was starting to get interesting, "I thought you had to go to the Import Store to get stuff from out of town."

That got a round of laughter.

"We're da *real* Import Store. But we're runnin' low since da last deal wen' bad."

"Sounds dangerous."

"Yeah, Tuesday our boys wen' out in the woods fo' da meetin', like normal. But dey shot Antwan, da King's driver. We ain't seen Luscious or Trung since den. Only King Death got outta der alive. Course, dat's why he da King."

Loki swallowed his next question as the bell attached to the top of the door rang. He didn't understand the locals well enough yet to know who it was safe to talk in front of. The man who walked in was wearing sneakers, denim overalls, a white t-shirt, and a straw hat. Sweat poured down his dirt cakes arms as he carried in a watermelon, "We's started the harvest. Willie, howsabout you gimme a beer fo' dis melon."

Willie jerked his thumb towards a pile of melons in the corner. "Michael, I got mo' dan I can eat already. One mo' ain't gonna help."

The man's face dropped, "Look Willie, I's been workin' hard today. You thin' you could run me a tab? Jus' until da market?"

Willie stared stone-faced at the watermelon picker; but Loki could tell he was about to cave in. Like everything else in town, the bar must be running on fumes; trying to get through until the next harvest. Willie couldn't afford to be generous, but at the same time Loki would guess Michael was a regular customer and friend. It looked like a good time for Loki to earn a little goodwill around town.

"Give the man a beer, I'll buy the melon."

"Thank ya, mister." Michael gave a slight bow to Loki. As he looked at Loki for the first time, confusion flashed across his face, "Whachu doin' in here?"

Loki looked at the pool cue in his hand, "I'm losing my shirt to these guys. Willie, could you slice that melon and pass it around to my friends?"

Willie took the watermelon, trying not to let his relief show, "I guess it's better den you eatin' all my peanuts."

Despite three beers, two slices of watermelon and who knows how many boiled peanuts, Loki found himself hungry for solid food as evening approached. Breakfast had been some flavorless nutrient bars from the gas station and some hot, flat cola masquerading as coffee. He paid his bar tab and billiard losses, and headed for the restaurant he had stopped at yesterday. He still didn't know the name of the place.

Loki would have expected more cars in the parking lot on a Friday night. The only vehicle was a truck jacked up to accommodate its oversized tires. A group of about half a dozen men in camouflage and orange vests was testing a spotlight attached to a swivel mount on the rack behind the cab.

As Loki pulled into a parking space and practiced how to say "I have Silvers" fast enough that Lucy wouldn't shoot him, an engine roared into the parking lot behind him. Instinct kicked in and Loki dove to the floor of his car to avoid the drive by shooting.

Instead of gunshots, he heard a car door open and someone, maybe Chris, yelling, "Bobby Cole! What the hell do you think you're doing? You drove that monster truck of yours through my field last night!"

"We can't help it if the deer decides to run through your field."

"Bullshit! You spun donuts out there! The harvest is this weekend! And you just ran over a fifth of my crop."

"Well since you sell the melons for nothing. Losing a fifth means you lost nothing."

"You son of a bitch!"

Loki recognized this sound: a brawl. No, this was a beating. He jumped out and sent a mental command to his car to pop the trunk. Loki could see it was Chris' truck idling behind him in the parking lot.

There, in the middle of the parking lot, a group of five guys in camouflage were kicking a figure curled up into the fetal position. Not content just kicking him in the back and guts, one of them, a short guy with black hair, was stomping on Chris' head. Chris alternated between low moans and sharp cries in time with

76

the heel pounding on his head.

Loki reached into his trunk and grabbed his shotgun. No one even noticed as he pointed it at the cab of the monster truck. He was a little disappointed the boom of the gun drowned out the crash of shattering glass. That got their attention. In the sudden silence he could hear the hiss of air escaping from a punctured tire.

"You just shot my truck." Even *he* couldn't believe what he just said.

"The way you guys run that truck around in the woods all night drunk," Loki raised the shotgun and rested it on his shoulder, "it's amazing the hunting accident didn't happen earlier."

"Why, you!" The ringleader charged him. Loki was guessing this was Bobby. The guy was already too drunk to charge a straight line. Loki didn't flinch until the hunter was just beyond arms' reach, then swung his shotgun, catching him in the head with the pump. The metal barrel would have hurt more, but Loki didn't want to risk damaging the barrel on that rock head.

The assailant went down in a pile at Loki's feet. Loki worked the pump to chamber another round and shoved the point into Bobby's groin.

"Oh, God! Oh, no! Please, no!"

"Clear out! Or idiot child here is going to have another 'hunting accident.'"

The others looked at each other. The guy who had stomped Chris' head broke rank first, running off into the darkness. The others followed at top speed.

Loki reached down and dragged Bobby to his feet. In the action he noticed the dark wet spot on the front of the hunting pants.

"Dude, did you just urinate on my gun? I don't know if I should shoot you or make you clean it."

"No, please. I didn't mean it." He grabbed a handkerchief out of his pocket and wiped down the barrel of the gun, "See. All clean."

"Good. Now start running, and don't stop until I can't see you." Loki tapped his temple. "And I have built in night vision."

After the crashing though the underbrush had faded into the distance, Loki walked over and pulled Chris to his feet.

"Thanks." He murmured through swollen, bloody lips.

"It's dinnertime, and watching an idiot get killed makes me lose my appetite."

"I should be getting home for dinner."

"No way. That right eye is going to swell shut in about 10 minutes; I can't let you drive like that. Come on, I'll buy this time."

"This place is closed."

Loki looked over at the building. Chris was right, the lights were off. Aside from his car and the two trucks, there were no other vehicles. It looked like dinner was going to be plastic wrapped nutrient bars from the gas station.

"Why don't you come to my place for dinner?"

"Okay, but I'm driving."

Loki sent wireless instructions telling his car to close the trunk and cranking the anti-theft shock system up to lethal voltage. He almost hoped those guys came back and tried to do something to his car. Then he realized, he had forgotten to put the shotgun back. The way his luck was going, he might need it anyways.

"Wait here until I come and get you," Chris warned. "My wife will freak when she sees you if I don't explain the situation first."

He stumbled out of the cab and staggered toward the house.

As time dragged on, Loki had the undeniable feeling that he was not alone. Cautiously he looked down from the pickup window. Eyes shined in the darkness below him. Loki had heard people used to keep dogs as pets, but his only personal experience had been with K-10, cybernetically augmented security animals, which had been trying to rip hunks of flesh out of him.

Loki scooted away from the door, then had the sinking realization that Chris had left his door open. He looked over, and there was a brown short hair dog with white spots, standing with its front two legs on the doorframe. It was close enough Loki could smell its breath.

Then the barking erupted. Every nerve in his body was screaming to start shooting and take off running. But Chris was the closest thing he had to a friend in this town, and Loki thought a dead dog or two might spoil that friendship. Of course getting eaten would also put a damper on things.

"Oh, hush! We know he's here." A woman with long blonde hair and a sleeveless t-shirt scooped the brown shorthair up into her arms, "Yes. You're a good dog. Thank you for telling us there's

78

a stranger here."

Mrs. Thompson couldn't hide her shock when she got a good look at Loki, but it only took her a moment to recover. "Let me throw these guys in the barn, and then we can go in and have some dinner."

Loki was too petrified to do anything except smile and nod.

Loki ate slowly, partially because he knew as the late arriving guest, everyone was eating light for his sake, and partially to savor the experience; crisp breading on the outside, juicy textured chicken on the inside, with a taste distinct from the outer layer.

"Thank you for saving my husband." Heather Thompson said as she passed a large metal mixing bowl piled high with hunks of broken watermelons across the table, "He just doesn't know what's good for him sometimes."

"I told you. I didn't go lookin' to fight. Just when I saw them there, I just kind of snapped."

The daughter, Rachael, had been staring at Loki all meal, "Are you really a big city ganger?"

Loki stopped mid bite and glared at her, "Watch it! I don't have a SID; I don't push drugs or make protection collections; I'm not tied down to a patch of turf and I don't take orders from the gang. I take dirty, dangerous jobs for hire. I'm an operative, not a ganger."

"But you're a member of a gang?"

"Well, yeah, the Tomb Rats watch my back, and I do some free jobs for them now and again, but... just don't call me a ganger again. It's different."

"I wish we could move to the city."

Loki caught the look from both Heather and Chris at the same time. He knew what they wanted him to say next, but it was what he would have said anyways, "Funny. I was just wishing I could move out."

"I'd better be going. It's getting late." Loki said as he finished up the last of his portion of the cornbread.

"Where are you staying?" Mrs. Thompson asked.

"I got a room at the Island."

"Oh, I can't let you stay in that dump, let me make up the sofa for you. Jimmy, go get the spare linens out of the closet."

"I'm not sure that is such a good..."

"Relax." Chris said, "I'll smooth things over with Frank about leaving your car in the lot overnight. He's been telling Cole and his gang to stop drinking in his parking lot for years. He'll love the story of how you sent them running."

"Lucy's the one I'm worried about."

"You're on your own with her." Chris laughed.

"You really should be taking it easy for a while with those injuries." Loki caught Chris as he tumbled down the stairs out of the house.

"Can't. The watermelon market is on Monday. After I take you back to your car, the whole family is going to spend all day pickin' 'em. I want get as much done as possible before the afternoon showers start."

Jimmy was muscling a wooden framework into the back of the truck to increase the carrying capacity. He wiped the sweat from his brow and gazed off to the south. "There's something good an dead out there today."

"How can you tell?"

"The buzzards." Jimmy pointed as a distant flock of black forms circling near the horizon, "It's probably just a deer the hunters didn't bother collecting."

"I'm pretty sure they didn't do any hunting last night."

Jimmy regarded him with annoyance. Loki could have pounded him into the dirt one handed, but Jimmy still wasn't going to cede any point, "Buzzards are funny. Sometimes they're right there waiting for something to die. Other times they'll let it sit for a week to get good an ripe before they show any interest."

"Any chance that thing could have died Tuesday night?"

"Well, yeah, maybe. I don't know when it happened."

"Tell you what. If you can lead me to that body, I'll spend the rest of the day helping you pick the melons."

Jimmy leaned out the window of Loki's car and looked up. "We're getting close now. We should be able to... ugh... we *can* smell it, now. I think it's roadkill around this bend."

After the curve, the road was blocked by a dated luxury town car painted with a flame pattern. Vultures perched on the roof, hood, and all but covered the ground around the car.

Loki turned off the igntion and before he could say, "You'd better wait here," Jimmy was out the door moving towards the flock.

"What? Did somebody freak out when they hit a deer and abandon the car?" Then Jimmy let out a holler of shocked disgust.

Loki walked up. The buzzards got out of his way but only hopped just beyond the reach of his kick and waited to continue their meal. There sprawled across the hood and hanging out the passenger window were the decomposing remains of two young black men. A gleaming, sliver cyber forearm lay on the hood, forgotten by the vultures now that they had eaten the flesh which had connected it to the elbow. Even Loki had a hard time not retching. He had dealt with bodies mummified in trunks and basements, but seeing people ripped open and eaten was a new level of disgusting. The worst part was, the way the ligaments held the bones together reminded him of dinner last night.

Regaining his composure, he looked at the bodies again, and could see that where they were lying was wrong for a drug deal gone bad. Their positions should have been more defensive. Either these guys were amateurs, or they had been ambushed.

Loki pulled out his pocket knife and moved back to the trunk. The buzzards closed in behind him, resuming their meal.

"What are you doing?"

"What does it look like? I'm picking the trunk."

"You know, the trunk release lever is just in there below the steering wheel."

Loki paused, unsure whether to slap Jimmy's smart mouth or thank him, "Well then reach in and pull it for me!"

"No way I'm putting my fingerprints on this thing!"

Loki walked forward, started to reach into the open driver's window, stopped and regarded his bare hand, then went back to his car and got a pair of gloves.

The trunk was crammed full of a spare tire, tire irons, baseball bats, handguns, ski masks, drugs, and dirty magazines. But like he was expecting, no silver. There was also no pneumonic pump and no place one would have fit.

"We've wasted enough time, Jimmy. Let's get going."

"We need to tell somebody about this." Jimmy settled onto the car seat. The heat and humidity made his bare skin stick to the synthetic leather.

"No. What we *need* to do is get your watermelons picked. These guys aren't going anywhere. When you get some spare time, you can lead the Sheriff out here so he can find the gun which killed James Morgan."

"What?!? How do you know that?"

"Street instinct. Now, what do I have to do to get a meeting with King Death?"

"Look, keep us out of anything to do with King Death. The closest I've ever gotten is seeing his car parked out front of the black church on Sundays."

That evening, Loki's entire body was sore from bending over to pick up the watermelons and hand them to Heather in the back of the truck. Despite the early start, they hadn't beaten the rain and he was now soaked to the skin with both sweat and rain. The moisture just aggravated the sunburn he had gotten in the morning and the mosquito bites he'd gotten all day long. He needed a tall, cold drink, and he knew that drink should be something other than beer, but he needed to go back to the bar. There were a lot more people than the last time he stopped in. The conversations stopped when walked in, and all eyes turned to him.

Loki scanned the crowd... he was in luck! "Jamal, how about another game of pool?"

"Sho, I'll take mo of yo money. But we'll have to wait fer a table."

Loki got a beer, a fistful of boiled peanuts and took a place at the bar next to Jamal. Now only half the room was staring at him, "So, Jamal, you going to church tomorrow?"

King Death was easy to spot. He was in his late twenties wearing a purple suit coat. Gold necklaces weighed down his neck and rings adorned every finger. His bodyguards filled the pews around him. The only one who stuck out more was Loki. It wouldn't have helped him blend in, but Loki wished he had brought a clean shirt with a collar from the city.

The Reverend Davis allowed his words to resonate in his throat, "It appears we have a visitor in our midst. Would you care to introduce yourself?"

Loki nudged Jamal in the ribs, "Dis is Loki. He's cool. He

82

jus got in too deep in da city and came out here ta let da heat blow over."

Loki stood up, "I'm just a poor sinner who sold his soul for 30 pieces of silver. I thought there might be others here trying to rid themselves of the taint of silver."

As Loki had hoped, King Death was waiting for him just outside the church. One of his henchmen held an umbrella over King Death, while getting rained on himself.

"Anybody ever tell you, you got a big mouth?"

"Lots of people tell me that, right before they do what I want."

"Get in da car."

"Thank you." Loki had to make do without an umbrella. He could have held his jacket over his head, but that would have revealed his under arm holster.

The hood of King Death's luxury town car had an elaborate airbrushing of a skeletal king sitting on a throne adorned with exotic animal pelts. Bikini-clad women wrapped their arms around each of his of his legs. The scene was underscored by the words "King Deth."

The backseat reeked cigarettes and other smoke.

One of the bodyguards got in behind Loki and took the center seat, pushing Loki to the far side. Finally King Death got in. The driver closed the door, folded up the umbrella, and circled around to the driver's seat.

As the town car started up, Loki reached out and contacted the wireless navigation system. The car was new enough that it still had all the factory default security protocols. All the autodrive functions were disabled, but he could hack his way in far enough to get the GPS records and see that the car had gone to the bank last Tuesday, then out into the woods.

"Give 'em yo gun." King Death pointed to the guard between them.

"What makes you think I'm carrying a gun?"

"I know yo packin' heat cause you ain't an idiot. And neither is I. Now, give 'em yo gun."

Loki did so.

"Now, whatcha want?"

"I just wanted to let you know that someone is trying to set you up. You didn't go to the bank to rob it; you needed silver to pay for the shipment you had coming in. But there's nothing illegal about trading in Silvers, why didn't you do it during daylight?"

"Sho, an why not tell Bubba when I got a shipment comin' in?"

"Oh, makes sense. But Slim wouldn't pay up, and things went South. But you didn't force the vault open. Bubba did that later so they could blame you. The Sheriff must be the only person in town with a jaws-of-life. And you certainly didn't carry out all that silver out in those two cars. Getting rid of everyone who could implicate you as an accessory to murder was a smart, if brutal, move. The fact that they're trying to frame you tells me you don't have the silver, but I'm betting you can give me a pretty good lead to track it down and clear your name."

"Well yo right Slim didn' wanna pay, but yo wrong we didn' take the silver. An e'rybody who knows dat all da silver is gone is dead now."

The bodyguard drew Loki's own gun on him.

Shoot me with my own gun to make it harder for the cops to trace, the thought flashed though Loki's mind as he wrestled the barrel away from himself. *And I fell for it like an idiot!*

But Loki wasn't a complete idiot. At a mental nudge the augmented driving system built into the windshield of the car burst into a fireworks display of color: driving directions to every major city on the globe, driving weather forecasts, menus to set the language and screen contrast, videos explaining the proper way to change a tire and check the fluid levels. The stereo blasted the German National anthem at full volume.

"What the..." The driver swerved erratically trying to see around the clutter.

Loki got his foot up on to the seat and was able to get his holdout gun out of the top of his boot. This was a fight he couldn't win. The door locks were still beyond the reach of his hacking, so he pointed over his shoulder and shot the window out behind him. Even though the main force of the blast was out, he still managed to get cut in the explosion of glass. The bodyguard took the shards to the face. That bought Loki just enough time to kick off and slide out the window.

His hair brushed the back tire as he rolled through the puddles along the side of the road. As soon as he could get his feet under himself, Loki took off into the woods. Even despite his own crashing and smashing through the undergrowth and the patter of countless rain drops on countless leaves, Loki could hear someone chasing after him. He only had one shot left in his snub-nose 9mm. That bodyguard had a full clip of 15 in Loki's gun, plus whatever else he was packing.

Loki reached out and contacted the only other wireless broadcaster in range: his car. He could drive his car remotely using the radar and thermal sensor without problem. Driving remotely while running full speed and dodging trees was a different matter. His own exertion and the swaying, drunken viewpoint of his car lurching down the road would have made him vomit, if there had been anything in his stomach. "Come on baby. Just keep tracking until the signal gets stronger."

The footsteps behind him stopped and... Loki felt the pain before he heard the triple-bang of burst fire. The sudden jolt knocked him forward, but his spinning feet pulled themselves under him. The left half of his back stung from the shoulder all the way down to the hip. That was good: it meant his armor jacket had stopped the round.

His car was blocked. There was a row of trees between the car and the direction of Loki's signal. That meant Loki had to go to it. He veered off to the right, heading straight towards the strongest signal. At least he could stop monitoring the car's sensors and concentrate on running. The footsteps behind him paused again.

Bang! Bang! Bang!

No pain. His pursuer was getting tired and falling behind. Loki dodged around another oak tree. It was thick enough that two people wouldn't have been able to link hands around it. More than thick enough to stop bullets, but more importantly it blocked the line of sight, at least for a moment.

After another 1000 feet to his car.

Loki slammed into a wire mesh fence before he even saw it. As fast has he was running, he rolled over the top without stopping. As he got to his feet, he found he had flipped over and was facing the woods.

Time for the Loki, the Trickster, to live up to his name. He fired into the woods, it was his last shot, he knew it wouldn't hit anything but he could hear the thug closing in behind him dive for cover all the same. He threw down the gun, ripped off his armored jacket and wrapped it around the nearest branch, snapping the collar button to keep it in place. Here in the open, the heavy thing would only slow him down anyways. Then he took off at a full sprint across the vegetable field. He ran between the rows of crops, not out of courtesy, but out of fear of getting tangled up in the zucchini vines. The soft wet ground sucked at his feet, trying to bog him down.

Behind him, he could hear his jacket getting shot full of holes.

His car sent him a security alert: radar echo, and heat source coming in fast on the driver's side. Just ahead, Loki could see the car on the other side of a row of trees lining the field.

"Warning," Loki could see in the radar echo a second heat source coming up behind him like a cornerback trying to run down a wide receiver on the way to the end zone. That guy just didn't give up.

This time Loki saw the fence and vaulted it. He mentally popped open the driver's door as he crashed through the trees. He took a bad step, then another, and flung himself head first into his car. The door slammed shut behind him. Loki put the car in drive as soon as he realized he had made it inside.

The car shook as the bodyguard disappeared from the radar. Thermalgraphic confirmed he had jumped onto the trunk. Loki activated the anti-theft shock pads: full voltage. There was a scream, a thud, and the burnt smell of ozone. Loki wondered if the guy had managed to hang on long enough to get a lethal shock. He wasn't going to stop and check.

Loki pulled himself up behind the steering wheel. He could drive better and faster using his own eyes. Up ahead, was a black car coming towards him, with the driver sticking his head out the window. Even from here Loki could hear the German national anthem.

Loki cranked the wheel to head down a side road, praying it wasn't a dead end. He strapped on his seat belt and stopped worrying about how deep the puddles were, just driving as straight as he could, as fast as he could. In the rearview mirror he saw King Death hanging out the back passenger side window with a submachine gun. Amateur. Sure it looked impressive, but the accuracy stunk at midrange. Still, thanks to the high rate of fire, King Death managed to skip a couple of shots off of the bulletproof rear window.

Loki kept the heavy equipment in the trunk, but he had a

surprise in the glove box for times just like this. He reached over and pulled out the silver canister. He rolled down his window, and waited for the next bend in the road. Just as he spun the corner, he pulled the pin and threw the canister out the window. A white teargas cloud mushroomed up behind him.

King Death's car rocketed out of the cloud and dropped a wheel into the water-filled retention ditch along the side of the road.

Loki drove full speed for another four bends in the road before he stopped and retrieved his assault rifle (with customized under-barrel grenade launcher) and shotgun out of the trunk. He also grabbed the combat knife and his heavy 'gunfight' armored jacket. He threw the weapons on the passenger seat, put on the jacket, so he didn't feel quite so naked and drove until he started picking up a wireless grid signal.

As Loki pulled into the highway truck stop, his mind was already scanning the menu and looking for an open table in the restaurant. His knife was the most concealable of the weapons he had left, so he strapped on, under his jacket even though he loathed hand-to-hand.

All the prices were listed in credit but he still flagged down a waitress on his way into the diner, "Excuse me. Do you take Silvers?"

He could see she was having a hard time believing that a chromed street punk had just asked her that, even if he was covered in mud. Finally she managed an indignant, "We don't take that counterfeit funny money. If you want something, pay in credit."

"Good answer!"

Loki sat down at a table in the back. If the adrenaline pumping through him wasn't enough to keep him awake all night, the coffee-flavored caffeine sludge he was swigging out of nervous habit would do the trick.

His only chance to get paid was to find the silver himself and take his 10% off the top. Screw the deal at this point. Loki knew Slim was in it up to his neck, but at this point he just wanted to know what happened to the silver to put his own mind at ease.

None of it made any sense. Despite what King Death said, there was no physical way to get a truckload of silver out with four (basically unaugmented) men and two cars. Since it hadn't been a planned bank robbery, they wouldn't have brought heavy vehicles or a jaws-of-life.

But then how did King Death know the silver was gone? And why was everyone who knew that dead? Why would King Death care if there was no silver in the vault?

...Because King Death knew if word got out the bank had been robbed, all the Silvers he had stashed away would be worthless. Slim had said there would be an uproar if people found out. King Death was willing to ice his own men to keep that secret. But then why rob it in the first place?

Loki didn't have any security footage, but he might as well have, the number of times he replayed the incident in his head: King Death walks in with his men; argues with Slim for a while; they shoot the guard; then the four drug dealers sprint out carrying an arm full of silver each; and the cars take off. He tried every possible variant on the scenario. No matter how he tried, it was just not possible to get a ton or two of silver out in a single trip. All night long Loki sat in the diner and watched the scene over and over in his mind's eye: they walk, in grab the silver, and run out. His head hurt from the repetition, watching over and over as they carried out an armload or two each time.

That was it! Loki the trickster had been the one tricked this time. It was time for some payback. He made the mental credit transfer to settle his bill, and braced himself for another trip into the dead zone.

The lack of sleep was starting to wear on Loki, but in a couple more minutes it would all be over. The market was abuzz with activity. Pickup trucks were backed up to conveyer belts. Families bucket-lined the watermelons out the back and onto the conveyer belt as fast as possible. Then a corporate inspector would glance at the fruit as it went past, occasionally reaching in to throw out one which wasn't up to his standards.

Slim Jones sat in the shade of one of the many semi truck trailers, ringed in by both sheriff deputies and corporate mercenaries. Off to the side of the market, a cluster of dated luxury cars were parked under a stand of giant oak trees. Loki noticed with a smile, the central, protected, car was different from the one King Death had been using yesterday.

Loki slung the assault rifle over his shoulder and grabbed his shotgun before walking into the market. Jamal started to wave at him from behind a battered red truck but Loki stared him down with an icy glaze and shook his head, then made a pointed look at King Death's car. Jamal swallowed hard and turned away, taking a melon-handoff from a plump middle aged woman in the back of the truck.

It was time for the big finale. Loki strode towards the secure little enclave where Slim was enjoying an iced tea, and got as close as he could until one of the deputies noticed him.

"The game's up, Slim! There's no silver in that vault!" Now that Loki had everyone's attention, no one was going to shoot him, at least until he finished talking, "You sold it all to King Death, little bit at a time, so he could buy drugs to push on people's kids. But rather than tearing up those Silvers that King Death traded in, you just kept using them. That bullet Morgan took was meant for you, and you deserved it. You've embezzled the entire economy, and now the silver's all gone. Then you and the Sheriff faked a robbery and called me in so King Death and me would kill each other."

Slim Jones swallowed hard and faked a laugh. He rose up out of his lawn chair with considerable effort and held his straw hat in front of himself, "Well, yeah, all the silver is gone. But if I hadn't kept a hold of those Silvers, the only person who would have any money left is that drug-pushing criminal. I can't believe that is in the people's best interest."

"But I want all of you to know, there is no reason we can't keep using Silvers. I'll still accept them at the Import Store."

Loki couldn't believe it; this part, at least, was a practiced speech.

"We'll even try to start stocking some silver coins in the Import Store for people who want them. Of course now that I don't have the reserve to help cover expenses, prices are going to have to go up."

A collective groan erupted behind Loki. He waited for the forward rush of the lynch mob. He was there, front and center to spearhead the push through the security line, all he need was the force of numbers behind him. The lynch mob never came. Sheriff Hunt gave Loki a glare that was worth 50 years to life.

The color drained from Loki's face. He beat a hasty retreat. Near the far end of the market he saw the Thompsons, picking up the melons out of the back of their truck and putting them on the conveyer belt feeding into the corporate trailer.

"Are people really just going to let him get away with that?"

Chris didn't even look up from his labor, "We could do something, but there's no guarantee it would make things better. In fact, I'll almost guarantee it wouldn't make things better."

Chris' bruised hands fumbled a melon. Loki caught it and put it on to the conveyer belt for him.

"The next fat-cat would be just as bad. I'll take the devil I know over the devil I don't."

Loki pulled into the Green Oak Bank just before closing. He left his weapons in the car, but the guard still drew on him when he walked in. The ATM glared at him.

"I just came to trade these in." Loki raised his hands over his head and shook a fist full of Silvers, "Or are you going to tell me they're completely worthless?"

The ATM held out her hand. Loki looked to the guard for approval and then walked up and placed the bills in her palm. He still kept his left hand over his head.

"We'll give you 25 credit for them."

"What? That's robbery! All right, all right, I'll take it. Just let me upload my account number." Again he glanced at the guard for permission.

When he connected to the system, the security barrier fell even easier than last time. The credit balance in the single account was 28,974 this time, but not for long. He froze the balance update function while he was making his credit withdrawal, then let it update just as he unplugged.

The ATM jumped out of her chair. She looked at Loki, not with disgust or hatred, but with pure animalistic fear. She sprinted back to the offices, "It's gone! It's all gone!"

Loki didn't think Slim could move as fast as he came lumbering out to check the screen for himself.

"Why, you!"

"Go ahead and shoot! Then you'll never get the credit back." Loki lowered his hands, "That money's already in Hong Kong and on its way to Zurich. Silver you can do with out, but when this credit-starved town learns you just lost everything they sold their crops for today, your life expectancy will be shorter than mine."

"What do you want?"

"When I was driving around, I saw a for-sale sign on the south side of town, down by the Island Motel."

"You're sayin' you want to move in?"

"I like it here. The food is good; the air is clean; I like the people... well most of the people." Loki started to walk around to get behind the counter, "I can always use another safehouse between operative missions. You're in desperate need of a computer security specialist; I'm thinking of applying for the job to make a little extra in my spare time. So if you'll just draw up a deed and a job contract we can make this nice and official."

Just as he passed in front of the guard, Loki lunged sideways, slamming his shoulder into the guard's chest and catching him against the wall. He gouged the guard's eye with his thumb for good measure as he spun to wrench the gun from his hand. It wasn't a clean move, they tumbled to the ground together but Loki landed on top and managed to come away with the weapon. He preferred automatics, but right now a revolver would have to do.

"I don't like having guns pointed at me." He told the guard as he stood up and put the gun in his under arm holster.

"You won't last a week," Slim sputtered. "Half the people in this town want to kill you."

"Wow, only half? Back home on the streets it's everybody. And you better not be one of them, because I'm the only one with the access codes to all those nasty little time bombs I just put in your computer system. Someone told me 'the devil you know is always better than the devil you don't.' You could have just faced the wrath of the people. They would have complained but nothing really would have changed, but in trying to hide your crimes, you invited in a devil that you know nothing about."

Children and Emperors

"What's all the commotion out there today?" Prime Minister Asayama asked without much interest, looking out the tinted limousine windows at the people shouting and waving banners. They ranged from street punks in ripped jeans and obscene t-shirts to Shinto priests in their baggy red pants and white gi shirts, all wearing headbands with the imperial symbol of a stylized chrysanthemum.

"It's a combination political party and religious sect," his aide, Kincha, said with equal apathy.

"What does this one want? Aside from to replace me with their leader."

"Actually, they don't want to replace you. They call themselves 'Followers of the Chrysanthemum.' They ask for the reinstatement of the Emperor."

Asayama groaned. He was in his early fifties and slightly overweight so groaning was easy, "This is the 22nd Century. Japan is a democracy. The last Emperor died without any male descendants almost fifty years ago. The Chrysanthemum Throne is vacant and on display for tourists. For most of history, the Emperor was little more than another decoration anyway."

"Should I roll down the window and let you tell them that?"

"Don't joke."

The crowd parted, but rather than allowing the limo to slip though and get the Prime Minister to his next appointment on time, a single man stood in the way. He wore black slacks and a black shirt with a high straight collar tight around his neck, and silver buttons displaced to the right. He was fully grown but young, made to look more so by his clothes, reminiscent of a high school uniform. His hair wasn't long, nor was it shaved in the traditional boys 'samurai haircut.'

He stood, feet planted at shoulder's width, arms folded as the car came to a stop in front of him.

"Driver, nudge him with the bumper and let's be on our

way," Asayama mumbled impatiently.

"I can't, sir," The chauffer sputtered.

"What? Why not?"

The driver reached into his pocket with a trembling hand and took out his wallet. He pulled out one of the newly minted 100 Yen bills and let the billfold drop to the seat besides him. Asayama took the money with curious disdain. Did his driver honestly think that he didn't know what it looked like? Before becoming P.M., he had been on the committee which had decided to use the Emperor's picture. He glanced down at the portrait of the final Emperor as a young man... or was it a picture of the man blocking the limousine?

Asayama stepped out of the car, "I'll grant that you know a good plastic surgeon."

Jeers rose from the crowd. The Imperial lookalike raised his hand, palm forward, to shoulder level and the crowd went silent.

"I am Tenriki, rightful heir to the Chrysanthemum Throne, and with it all of Japan." His voice was too booming for his short stature and small frame. "I do not begrudge you, nor anyone else in the government, your place. My family has always had assistance administrating the realm. But you need to remember and do honor to the source of your power. I'm here to remind you."

"You're over one hundred years behind the times." The P.M. chided like a history teacher would a forgetful student. "The Emperor was made a figurehead at the end of Part Two of the World War. As for you, every so-called bastard son to come forward has failed the genetics test, and you're too young to even claim that!"

"If you want genetic proof, I can give it to you."

A shot glass from the mini-bar floated out of the limo's still open door. Aide Kincha jumped. Asayama wanted to jump, but thirty years of politics had given him a poker face. Psionic activity was, after all, a well documented and somewhat understood phenomenon, if not an everyday occurrence.

The skin over Tenriki's outturned palm ripped open. A stream of blood flew across the intervening space and filled the glass. The cut on his palm closed itself like a zipper, leaving no mark.

"Take that blood to any geneticist you like. Have them run every test of which they can think. They will tell you what I have told you. The two heavenly rice fields have already been grown. My

93

followers are harvesting rice for the coronation banquet. You have 72 hours to hand over the Imperial Palace, so that we may begin construction of the banquet halls." With that, he turned and walked into the crowd, which parted respectfully, and closed behind him. The shot glass of blood came to rest in Kincha's hand.

"Mr. Prime Minister, Tanaka Kazu of the Department of Public Health to see you," Kincha called, opening Asayama's office door.

Asayama didn't look up from his paperwork, "Please take a seat, Dr. Tanaka." After he heard Dr. Tanaka settle into one of the padded leather chairs in front of the desk, Asayama continued, "Which is slowly killing the populous this time, the water or the air?"

"Actually, sir, this is about the blood sample you sent us."

Asayama put down his pen and looked up. Tanaka's short cropped black hair was moist with sweat. He held a file folder with a white-knuckle grip and stared back at the Prime Minister from behind small wire-rim glasses.

"You would have just e-mailed me the results unless you had found something. Is that nutcase the product of frozen semen someone forgot to tell us about?"

"No sir, the genetic profile is too close to that of the Emperor."

Asayama rocked back in his chair and put his hands on his face, "A mature, full term clone? What a legal nightmare. And of the Emperor to boot!"

"The nightmare isn't just legal."

"What?"

"The genetic match isn't within the margin for a clone, so I decided to investigate the areas of difference. He has active psy sites."

"Oh, that's right. Psychics have different genes."

"Not different genes, different shaped genes." Tanaka corrected, "Nucleotides are composed of incredibly complex chemicals that can take on virtually any shape. Very few of the shapes are actually viable. It's only been in the past thirty years that we've learned that when an alternate shaped gene is located at specific sites, psychic abilities manifest. The more active sites, the more powerful the psychic."

94

"That's right. The military calls those five things they grew from test-tubes experiments 'Threes' because they have three active sites apiece."

"The military has half a dozen Threes?"

Asayama stopped short, "Don't repeat that to anyone. But what is this new guy? A rouge Three?"

"No, sir. No Three," he added a caustic qualifier, "that we've been told about, has ever lived past puberty."

"Then tell me what he is!" Asayama leaned over his desk and screamed.

Tanaka closed his eyes and took a deep breath. "He's a Forty Nine."

"What?" The P.M.'s voice was barely a whisper.

"Tenriki has 49 of the 103 known sites active. His DNA is so mangled, I don't know how it holds itself together, but somehow the oddities manage to cancel out, making semi-normal looking chromosomes."

"What's the short version?" Asayama's entire body felt numb. Whispering that single sentence took all of his strength.

Tanaka reached into his pocket and produced a wadded up handkerchief. He unfolded it, revealing a shot glass whose interior had a red tint, "There has been one other cup like this in the history of the world, and the Christians are still looking for it. Either we can meet his demands, for the rest of his life, or we can determine who made him and ask for the kill-switch."

"The what?"

"It's standard practice in genetic warfare to give your creations an Achilles Heel you can exploit if they turn against you."

Asayama sat up straight again, "Tell me more about kill-switches."

Neither man noticed the blood residue twitch in the glass.

Tenriki sat lotus style in the sanctuary of his combination temple and political headquarters. He contemplated the numerous puncture wound scars on the inside of his left elbow and counted the hours to his next shot. It could be disastrous if anyone other than Dr. Gensha learned of his weakness. "I don't like the way this conversation is going," he whispered. "Little Ones, would you tell the good minister he is displeasing me."

Angel was a Two. You wouldn't have been able to tell, as her only outstanding feature was her military buzzcut black hair. Two decades ago, everyone had been calling her a genetic 'Super Psychic' vastly more powerful than the naturally occurring Ones. But when she had been seven years old, a zygote with three Psy-sites grew into an embryo for the first time. At that time, her training had changed radically. Rather than being a super soldier, she was to become a nanny for the Threes, just as she had been raised by Ones. Angel was now twenty-five years old. If the causality list from last year's failed revolt in China was correct, she was the oldest Two in the world. Even though she was technically enlisted, her only duty was caring for Japan's Threes. It wasn't that her limited telekinesis gave her any power over the Threes, but her abilities gave her a glimpse of the world in which the Threes lived.

Sakura, an eight year old girl, trotted up, her silk-fine amber hair almost floating on the air. Her hazel eyes were blood shot, as always, and her white play dress helped disguise, but couldn't completely hide, the fact that she was skeletally thin.

"Angel?" she asked in a cheerful, high-pitched little-girl voice. "Could you please call the Prime Minister and tell him that he's making the Emperor mad?"

Angel gave a sad smile. Sakura's postcognitive abilities let her read past events from places and objects. Because she could see clearly how the past had led up to the present, she was remarkably good at predicting the near future. But because of her abilities, she had little to no concept of time.

"Sakura, that's the Past, dear."

Angel grunted from the psychic equivalent of a gut punch. Reflexively, she lashed out the only way she overpowered the Threes: Physically. Coming to her senses, she stopped just short of slapping Sakura's face. Bruising Sakura meant weeks of coagalative shots to keep her from bleeding to death under her skin. Sakura didn't flinch. Was it because she knew Angel wouldn't slap her this time, or was it because she didn't care?

"I forget that others are trapped in time," Sakura said indignantly, "but Emperor Tenriki understands and helps me."

She smiled again, "Thank you for calling."

With that she skipped back to her dolls.

Angel leaned her back against the brightly-colored nursery wall. She wasn't sure what that conversation meant, but Sakura was right: She was going to call the Prime Minister.

Asayama didn't so much put the phone down as have it fall out of his trembling hand, "He's got one of our Threes working for him."

"Checkmate?" Tanaka asked, resigned.

"Perhaps not." Asayama leaned forward pressing his fingertips together. He had faced political checkmate three times in his career. The solution had been the same each time: Give the opponent enough rope and let him hang himself. "This guy obviously thinks he can take on an army single handedly, so we'll let him. I'll tell him to prove his power to Parliament, I need him to take on a dozen elite units and our Psy-Corp."

"And if he wins?"

"Then I've done nothing to oppose him and he still has no reason to begrudge me my job." He picked up the phone and dialed the psy nursery.

"Hello, Psyward? Get all the Threes ready for a battle tomorrow."

"Could you repeat that?" Angel asked, "I couldn't hear you over Bara."

"I didn't hear anything."

"Bara's a telepath. Her words come straight into my brain, trampling whatever was there at the time."

"I said get ready to deploy the Threes tomorrow. Once we've determined where to stage—"

"It's been decided." Angel interrupted.

"What?"

"That's what Bara wanted to say. She said she'll play your war game, but only if it's in Tokyo so you can't use the 'big mushroom bomb' (I think she means nuclear warhead) you're thinking about. She also says that Emperor Tenriki agrees to your terms, and if possible he'd like to have a light lunch with the Threes beforehand."

Asayama swallowed hard. He just had to brazen this situation out, like he had the others, "Very well, we'll start at thirteen hundred hours, so if the five of them show up about twelve hundred—"

"Four, sir," Angel interrupted again. "Kiku died in her sleep this morning."

"Why wasn't I told?"

"I filed the reports. I guess they just haven't reached you yet. This wasn't unexpected, she was fourteen years four months and three days today."

Angel listened to ninety seconds of unnecessary instructions and let the Prime Minister hang up on her. The rest of today was going to be busy. She had to get the Threes ready for a rare trip out of the nursery and falsify backdated reports, but first she owed Kiku an explanation.

Angel walked towards the back of the playroom, dodging to one side of a building block castle floating in the air. The castle interposed itself again.

"Momo, not now."

Momo leaned forward, resting his hands and chin on the hilt of his toy sword floating in front of him. He wore nothing but a pair of red shorts, which only accented his blotchy skin. He stared condescendingly at her, even though his brown eyes were always watering. His long black hair beat the hypersensitive skin on his back like a thousand whips, "Give me what I want, and I'll let you go see Big Sis."

"I said not now!" Angel thrust the blocks aside with her mind.

The castle fell apart and the blocks took new trajectories, zipping in circles around Angel at a blurring speed. She reached out and a wooden block struck her hard in the back of the hand. She tried to deflect the blocks with her mind, but there were too many. Momo could compensate faster than she could clear a path.

Angel took a deep breath and braced herself to walk through the onslaught. The wooden building blocks burst into flames around her. The breath came out as a sigh.

"I'll give you two CCs of psy booster when the battle starts, no sooner."

"Three."

"Three? Do you want to burn yourself out?"

"You've seen Big Sis." Momo jerked his head towards the back wall, "If my options are burnout or end up like her, I'll take four CCs."

"You're getting two," Angel said, "or none at all if I get hit by one more block."

The flames went out and the charred blocks fell to the floor around Angel's slippers, "You promised me two CCs, Two. Don't forget."

Angel snarled, but held her tongue. You couldn't inflict the powers of a Three on children and expect them to remain well balanced, but Momo was the worst of the lot.

Angel swallowed down her anger before opening the door in the back wall to what was euphemistically referred to as "The Big Kids' Room." Actually, it was an intensive care ward to keep the Threes alive as long as possible.

Two of the beds in the room were empty. The third was surrounded by machines. A young girl lay in the bed, her long white hair soaked in sweat. Her eyes were clouded over, so that the irises and pupils were no longer discernable. The swollen eyeballs bulged out of their sockets so much that the lids could not close, even for a blink. Her skin was deathly white, her lips ice blue.

This slowly dying shell was all that remained of Kiku. She wore a middle school uniform: blue pleated skirt, white shirt with a red ribbon tied around the collar, and a blue jacket. White socks and black buckle shoes completed the outfit. Shoes, even brand new ones, were dirty things, and Kiku shouldn't have been allowed to wear them in bed. But if she didn't wear them now, she never would.

Kiku had always been blind and deaf, but her mind could see and hear far beyond the walls of the underground nursery. Even though she had never attended a day of school physically, she knew that receiving a middle school uniform was an important rite of passage for girls her age. A month before, she had requested one for herself.

Angel had been so heartbroken at the request that she had had Bara transfer Kiku's vision of the perfect uniform to her own brain before going shopping. Kiku had been so weak by then that all she could do was finger the fabric. Now she couldn't even do that, so every day Angel dressed her in a clean uniform and washed the old one.

Angel sat down in the chair by the bed, "You're too weak to fight and that political idiot doesn't realize you can be that weak without being dead. So I explained it in a way he could understand."

"Only the body is weak," Kiku whispered without turning her head.

"Don't talk. Have Bara relay it. Save your strength."

"For what?"

Tears formed in Angel's eyes.

"You could lose..." Kiku's lips kept moving, but no more sound came out.

"I could lose my job. But that job is to protect you, so I have to do it."

"...your life."

"I still have to do it." There was no point in sugarcoating things for the Threes. They already understood the world better than she did.

"Why?"

"You can't attend the lunch like this," Angel glanced at the half full IV bag, "so you can't attend the battle either. Those are the rules."

Kiku gave a weak and short lived smile. "Scared."

"It's okay to be scared. Death scares me, and you're closer than I am." Angel didn't even try to stop her tears now.

"Threes die violently. I... different."

"You're getting tired." Angel stood, wiping her eyes. "We'll talk some more after you've rested."

"Please... later... might... dead..."

Angel sunk back into the chair, "Should I tell you a story?"

"Yes... please..."

Angel took a deep breath, and gathered her thoughts. A tale from the Kojiki, Japan's oldest written record came to mind first, "Now is long ago. Susa-no-Wo, the God of Storms and the Sea was upset because he couldn't see his mother, Izanami, because she had crossed over to the land of the dead. To distract himself he decided to pay a visit to his sister, Amatarasu-Omikami goddess of the sun. There was a great stir in heaven when they heard Susa-no-Wo coming because he was a swaggering, boisterous warrior-god. Amatarasu-Omikami went out to meet her brother on the road. She took up her bow and arrows and wrapped stings of... What's the name? The smooth stones carved to look like the American number nine?"

"Magatama."

"Shh, you're supposed to be resting." Angel continued, "So

Amatarasu-Omikami wrapped stings of magatama gems around her body, armed herself with a bow and arrows and waited for her brother on the road to Heaven. Before long Susa-no-Wo approached. 'It is good to see you sister. I've come to pay you a visit,' he called out.

"'Don't come any closer. We don't want any trouble in Heaven,' she yelled back, notching an arrow.

"'But I haven't done anything,' he protested. 'Prove your intentions,' Amataratsu-Omikami demanded. Susa-no-Wo replied, 'Let's swear oaths and bear children.'

"Now, as gods they didn't bear children in the normal way." Angel stopped. Both Kiku and herself had come into existence in a test-tube. Her own odds of having children were slim and Kiku's were nonexistent. What meaning did 'the normal way' have for them?

Kiku shifted slightly in the bed, snapping Angel from her thoughts, "As I was saying, to bear children they went to the Celestial Well. Amataratsu-Omikami took her brother's sword, broke it into seven pieces and chewed them. She took a mouthful of water from the well, mixed it with the sword pieces, and spit out the mixture in a fine mist. From that mist a host of minor deities were born. Susa-no-Wo took a string of his sister's magatama beads, chewed them to bits, took a drink from the well, and spit the mixture. He also gave birth to a group of deities, all of whom were female. This was seen as a good omen and Susa-no-Wo was allowed to enter Heaven.

"Once in Heaven, Susa-no-Wo immediately started turning the place upside down. He ran and shouted, scaring the other gods. He defecated in the palace and broke down the divisions between the rice fields. Seeing his behavior, Amataratsu-Omikami decided her brother must be drunk and thought nothing more of his actions.

"One day while Amataratsu-Omikami was in her weaving room, Susa-no-Wo killed the Heavenly Piebald Donkey and skinned it with backwards skinning." Angel repeated from memory. The significance of the donkey and the definition of backwards skinning had been lost to the eons, "He drug the bloody carcass onto the roof of his sister's spinning hut, peeled back the thatch and threw the body of the donkey inside. Amataratsu-Omikami's assistant was so startled she struck herself with the weaving shuttle and died.

"Angered and shamed by her brother's behavior, Amataratsu-Omikami secluded herself in a cave. Remember, Amataratsu-Omikami was not only the highest goddess but also the sun goddess, so her retreat plunged the Heavens into darkness. The other gods hatched a plan to bring her out of hiding. First, they took a large mirror and hung it in front of the cave. Then they held a party outside the cave. Amataratsu-Omikami heard the signing and laughing and her curiosity overcame her shame. 'Why are you celebrating?' she called outside. 'We're celebrating because there is a goddess who is greater than you out here,' the gods called back.

"Amataratsu-Omikami had never seen a goddess greater than herself, so she had to take a look. When she peaked outside she saw a goddess more beautiful and radiant than any she had ever seen. Amataratsu-Omikami stepped forward to get a better look at the goddess staring back at her, for she had never seen a mirror. As soon as she was outside, the other gods sealed the cave to prevent her from retreating again."

Angel paused for breath, "The epilog is that it was decided Susa-no-Wo had to be punished for his shameful behavior, so he was banished down to Earth."

Kiku's lips moved with visible difficulty, "Does she... still... love... hiii..."

The question caught Angel off guard; the Kojiki was just a collection of stories. She had never tried to guess the emotions of the characters. How could she guess how Amataratsu-Omikami felt about her brother? Angel didn't have a brother, or a sister for that matter. Even her parents had been terrified of her, "I don't know about goddesses, but if I had a brother, I'd love him no matter what he did."

Angel stood and started to turn. leaving Kiku lying peacfully. A whisper stopped her in her tracks, "Why... my... name..."

"I wish I could give you a reason, like how Bara's skin is bright red so we named her after the rose. But I can't. We give the girls Japanese flower names and the chrysanthemum seemed as good as any at the time."

"Always... reason... but... not... understa..."

Angel leaned closer, trying to read her lips. Kiku wasn't trying to say anything; she was panting for breath. Angel laid the oxygen mask over Kiku's face.

"I'm sorry. I'm sorry!" She ran out of the Big Kids' Room crying. Kiku was right. The other Threes had died violently. The first Japanese Three had died coughing blood, the second screaming when her stomach burst and the acid dissolved her organs, the last ran into a wall and broke his neck. Angel had mourned each of them in turn, but the way Kiku was wasting away, not so much dying as ceasing to be alive, was more than Angel could bear.

The Threes had long ago stripped Angel of her privacy, so rather than run and hide, she flung herself down in a corner and curled into the fetal position. Today was going to be busy. She had to prepare the Threes for tomorrow and forge some backdated reports, but first she had to have a nice long cry.

The helicopter carrying the Threes touched down in Ueno Park. Two soldiers with patches on their shoulders indicating that they were Twos leapt out first and pointed their assault rifles at the lone figure standing in front of the concrete pond. Tenriki wore the same outfit as when he had confronted Asayama, but now with a long cape, waving and snapping in the wind from the helicopter.

"We haven't started yet." Tenriki said disdainfully and the magazines fell out of two guns pointed at him, "Would you leave us alone? I invited Angel and the children, not you."

"Do what he says." Momo strode up behind the soldiers. He was much more presentable now, wearing a loose, white martial arts uniform with his wild hair tamed into a long braid, "We'll be fine."

The two men glanced at each other, then back at Angel who was disembarking the helicopter with the infant Ume, latest of the Threes, held close to her chest, "We'll be fine."

Angel half closed her eyes and the ammo clips floated off the ground, allowing the soldiers to grab them and retreat to the helicopter without the indignity of kneeling to retrieve them.

"In a short while, you will be ordered to attack me. I can not in good conscience ask you to disobey your orders, but for the time being we should be cordial." Tenriki said as the helicopter lifted off, "The children have informed me of their dietary restrictions, and boxed lunches have been prepared accordingly. If you would follow me."

Angel wanted to be suspicious, to be furious, that he had

103

subverted the Threes, but she couldn't. The four children around her were completely comfortable with the situation, even anxious for their first picnic. It was her karma to live perpetually in abject defeat.

"But you are not defeated," Tenriki smiled at her. "This is not an invasion. It is a restoration."

Complete, perpetual, abject defeat.

The party arrived at a blanket spread out on the ground with six stacks of lacquered boxes and a cheap throw-away plastic tray for short-order boxed lunches.

Angel looked at the food in the plastic tray and spun to face Tenriki, fire in her eyes. Ume, still in her arms, gave her a mental nudge, protesting the sudden movement.

"It's for Sakura." Tenriki explained, "You have a lacquered set, just like the rest. I thought the new materials would be much easier for Sakura to use, rather than something layered with past impressions."

Angel looked back to the lunches. The children were already settling themselves on to the blanket. "There's an extra lunch."

"For Kiku." Tenriki sat down on the blanket and took off his shoes, "She couldn't attend physically, but she knows the look, smell and taste better than you would if you ate it."

"Kiku's dead." Angel said flatly.

"Ah, yes." he smiled, "Then I am being a sentimental fool and must be humored."

"You mean ask to be humored." Angel sat down, laying Ume on the ground besides her. The Threes all cringed, physically and mentally.

"The Emperor does not ask and is not corrected." Tenriki spoke in a tight voice.

Angel braced herself. She felt the approach of a mental blow more powerful than any the Threes had landed in their worst tantrums.

Momo leapt to his feet and pointed an accusatory finger at Tenriki, "You have to follow the rules too! We came to lunch as friends. If you have to punish the Two, do it during the fight. But right now the food is getting cold."

The two males locked gazes. Tenriki was the first to look away, "The food is getting cold."

There was a hearty round of "Itadakimasu" expressing

gratitude for the food in Japanese, and they began eating.

As Angel helped the Threes back into the helicopter, Tenriki surveyed the rows of tanks, troops and artillery ringing in Ueno Park, "I knew it would come to this sometime. I will try not to hurt the children too badly, but I can't promise anything for the others."

Angel paused, thought about what Tenriki had said, then climbed into the helicopter herself.

Tenriki sighed, somehow making himself heard above the routers, "Thank you for not commenting. You are mastering the art of being a good subject. But you are right: there are still things I can't do."

Angel slid the door closed without a word. Bara was the first to 'speak.' *Don't point the big guns at him. Between the time the gun is pointed and when it's fired, he'll move. Instead shoot everywhere in the park at once.*

Angel looked at the scene of complete devastation that used to be Ueno Park. The scene behind her was not much better. Sakura was hiding under an ambulance, holding her head, crying at the top of her lungs. Bara sat on the ground playing listlessly with a plush dog she had brought along. Ume was asleep (or knocked out) kicking in a nightmare. Momo was on his hands and knees covered in sweat and panting for breath. The red spots on his skin had burst into open sores, adding blood to the film coating his body.

"I can still win," Momo croaked. "Give me a shot of Gamma and I can win."

"But..."

"It will kill me in ten seconds, but I can kill him in nine if you shoot me up."

Asayama crawled out the top hatch of an overturned armored troop transport, "Did he just say he has a way to win?"

"No," Angel spun to face the Prime Minister. "He's become suicidal. He just asked for a potent neural toxin."

"They call it a neuron accelerator." Momo called, "I don't know what that means, but I know the psychic mice go through the roof when you give it to them."

"And then they die." Angel interjected.

"Give him the drug." Asayama ordered.

"What?"

"We've lost. If this gives us a chance to win we have to take it. Now carry out your orders, soldier."

The helmet floated off the head of a downed serviceman nearby. It hovered in the air for a moment, then threw itself into Asayama's face, knocking him to the ground.

Angel strode to the ambulance and carefully drew one CC out of a vial labeled only with the Greek symbol 'gamma' into a hypodermic syringe. She recapped the syringe and walked to Momo. She knelt down besides him, "Momo, I'll give this to you, but only if you look me in the eyes and tell me it's what you want."

Momo raised his head and made eye contact, but said nothing. He looked out over the park. Tenriki was striding towards them. His body showed no sign of the numerous wounds which had reduced his shirt to bloody rags. His tattered cape, still on fire in places, twitched spasmodically in the wind.

Momo looked back to Angel, "Good or bad, this is the way things are. Give me the shot!"

Angel couldn't argue with that tone of voice. She uncapped the syringe and took Momo's left arm. She bit her lip and drove the needle into a vein on the inside of the elbow.

"You're either a very brave or a very stupid young man." With that she pushed down the plunger. Momo leapt to his feet, muscles tensed. His braided hair flew apart, flying around him as if in a violent wind. His lips pulled back in an insane grin, showing his teeth locked together. His eyes bulged like Kiku's.

Tenriki dropped to his knees, hugging his arms around his chest. The would-be-Emperor panted loudly. He threw his head back and screamed in agony.

Blood started to trickle, then run out of Momo's nose. His eyes closed, his muscles slackened and he fell backwards.

"Ten seconds exactly." Angel muttered bitterly.

Tenriki rose to his feet, "Momo was a worthy adversary, and given time he would have defeated me. But he didn't have that time."

Angel just stared at the body as Tenriki came up to her, "There are others who need your help more. See to them."

Turning to Asayama who was picking himself up off the ground he continued, "Now, good minister, if you will officially sign

106

over the palace to me, my people can begin construction of the ceremony halls."

"There have been many palaces. Aren't your priorities in the wrong places?" Sitting on a stone, downhill from where the Threes had been based, was a young woman with bright blue eyes, ruby red lips, and long white hair.

Angel gazed at the fair skinned girl in disbelief, but the middle-school uniform left little doubt, "Kiku!"

"Who are you?" Tenriki shrieked.

"I should ask the same question to a man who calls himself 'Emperor' without a single Regalia."

"Soon, I will be presented with the Imperial Jewels and the Imperial Sword. The mirror is at the Imperial shrine in Ise. Now that I've proven my power, the country will give me what I'm entitled to."

"Entitled to?" Kiku shook her head.

"The sun goddess Amatarasu-Omikami gave the three Regalia to her grandson, the first Emperor. They have been passed down through my family to every Emperor. I am Emperor, they are mine!" Tenriki's voice cracked in hysteria. His fists turned white as they shook at his sides.

"And if someone stops you from obtaining them?" Kiku asked bemused.

"Like who?"

Tenriki flew backwards, slamming into a tree as thick as his leg. There was a creak followed by a groan as the tree fell, with Tenriki laying on top of it.

"Me."

Tenriki sat up and cleared his head. He stared at Kiku for a moment. The shattered pavement stones, from pebbles up to rocks the size of Kiku's head, rose off of the ground around her and pelted her. The onslaught tossed her about like a doll. She rose off the ground, supported by nothing but the rocks striking her underneath.

"Stop it!" Angel screamed and ran towards Kiku.

Behind her there was a crack. The rocks fell out of the air, and Angel lunged just in time to catch Kiku in her arms. The girl was covered with cuts and bruises, her precious uniform torn to bits.

Angel looked back to Tenriki. The end of the fallen tree had splintered, and he had eight large wooden shards sticking in him.

He sat wide-eyed with his mouth hanging open and saliva running out. Even with her limited knowledge, Angel recognized the significance of the wounds: Chakra points.

Kiku slipped from Angel's arms, dropping to her feet. Once supporting her own weight, she brushed herself off. As her hands passed over her body, the tears in the uniform fixed themselves, missing pieces reappeared. The cuts and bruises vanished.

Kiku turned around, "Angel, would you please give the blood on your hands to Dr. Tanaka. I'm sure he'll find it interesting."

"Now," she spun to face Tenriki, "if you'll start acting like an Emperor instead of a barbarian king, I'll give you a chance to earn the Chrysanthemum Throne. We're only children, so you'll have to play a simple game we already know: keep away. If you can get one of the three Regalia before we can, I'll recognize your right to be Emperor."

The wooden stakes withdrew themselves from Tenriki's flesh, leaving oozing holes. "And if I don't accept your terms?"

"This is not a list of terms. It is a test. You can pass or fail." She turned her head, "Little Brother, will you help me?"

"You know I love a good fight." Momo said, walking over. His face was free from rashes and sores for the first time, letting his East-Asian complexion show.

"Will you behave yourself?"

"Don't I always?"

Kiku glared at him.

He sighed, "I promise to behave."

"Then let us begin."

Kiku's and Momo's bodies started glowing. Their features became indistinguishable. They were simply two child shaped light sources. The lights went out and there was nothing left. Tenriki lifted himself from the pile of splintered timber and ran to the South.

Angel stood motionless.

Dr. Tanaka is in the army-car Asayama got out of, Bara thought to her.

"What?" Angel unnecessarily mouthed the word.

The man you're supposed to give the blood to, Bara explained, *After that, can we go back to the nursery? It's not fun here anymore.*

108

Tenriki ran as hard as he could. He also sent out a mental message to a nearby bosozoku, bike gang, whose members included Followers of the Chrysanthemum. He needed to get to the Imperial Palace fast, and they were his best bet.

Tenriki was honestly scared. He knew of every powerful psychic in the world, from the tribe of pigmy Ones to the closely guarded American Four, but he had never sensed anything like that girl. Quite literally never, even when she threw him against the tree, all he felt was the impact, not the psychic energy used to pushed him. Had Dr. Genshi somehow concealed the existence of another Forty Nine from him? The doctor only wanted to use Tenriki as a puppet Emperor, why would he hide the competition? Regardless of what that girl was, or why she had decided to oppose him, he had to take her seriously.

An aerodynamic racing motorcycle passed Tenriki, then slowed down, allowing him to vault onto the back. Only then could he spare the concentration to close his wounds.

There was a long line of black diplomatic sedans waiting at the small guardhouse and the simplistic but sturdy black metal gate leading to the Imperial Palace. The red racing bike which Tenriki was riding, along with a dozen other brightly colored bikes, rocketed past the cars. A volley of sparks erupted out of the gate's electric motor and the barrier slid sideways, just before the first bike and its clashingly-brightly colored rider reached it.

The police at the guardhouse stood slack-jawed as one bike engine after another whined over the bridge to the far side of the moat.

Like a high speed parade, each gaudy biker tipped his bike and leaned low, almost touching the ground to bank around a right angle in the road. Tenriki leaned into the turn, following the mental impressions of his driver.

The convoy squealed up the tortuous winding road. At any other time in history, they would have been beset by imperial guards at every curve, but at any other time in history they wouldn't have been going 100 kph.

The cycles flew past the wooden front doors of the palace proper and Tenriki vaulted from the seat, using telekinesis to soften his landing. He sent out a mental message to his escorts, "Thank you for your help. I know what you're thinking, but this is my house now. Vandalize it, and I'll kill you."

Tenriki's mind had roamed the rooms and halls of the palace so often, he didn't notice that this was the first time his body entered. He stopped, panting for breath, at the entrance to the wing holding the Regalia.

A small gesture of his hand caused the sliding paper-walls to move aside, turning the series of rooms into a long hall. At the end of the corridor was a decorative screen painted with turtles, cranes, carp, and of course chrysanthemums.

The priceless screen shuddered and fell to the straw tatami mat floor. On the altar behind it were the two of the Imperial Regalia: The Imperial Jewels, a necklace strung with magatama, and the Imperial Sword, a long straight blade inscribed with ancient Chinese characters.

Tenriki sighed with relief, then balked. He knew the logical thing to do was race to the altar, but the only time you wore shoes while walking on tatami mats was when carrying out a body after a wake. It wouldn't be proper to enter without removing his shoes. Besides, that white haired lass might disqualify him if he broke the taboo.

He lifted his feet and flicked off his shoes. As the second shoe hit the floor, something caught his eye and he looked down. There was a pair of polished black shoes set politely to one side, toes pointed towards the door. Tenriki's head snapped up, his juvenile tormentor was skipping down the hallway in her white socks.

Tenriki sprinted, although he was still winded from his dash to the palace. His lungs burned, his legs ached. He pushed his body to its limits, then used his mind to push beyond the limits. The race lasted forever, but was over in an instant. Kiku reached the altar just before him. As her hand closed around the Imperial Jewels, Tenriki lunged onto the table. He crashed over it, into the wall and on to the floor.

He leapt to his feet, holding the sword in a ready position. Kiku had the Jewels around her neck. She examined them, apparently unaware of the sword pointed at her.

"I did it! I have a Regalia, The Sword."

"No you don't." Kiku said disinterested. With that, the sword turned to dust in Tenriki's hands.

With a yelp, he dropped to his knees and scooped up two fist-fulls of the powder, "How could you? This was one of the treasures passed down from the gods."

"It was a cheap copy."

"That's right." Tenriki remembered, "The real sword was kept at Ise until the head priestess gave it to a samurai to take on his campaign. After winning, he enshrined the sword at Atsuta Shirne in Nagoya."

"You should make that your next stop." Kiku walked away.

"Where are you going?"

"To get my shoes. I suggest you do the same. Little Brother has already gone after the Sword."

"What's taking so long?" Asayama burst into the genetics lab, "You said it would take three hours to analyze the DNA. That was five hours ago."

Tanaka looked up from his desk annoyed, "Yes but that doesn't include the time to cross correlate the data with the information you just sent over about the military Threes and..."

"And?"

Tanaka put his hands, still in latex gloves, against his forehead, "The results don't make any sense. This blood didn't come from a living creature. The DNA is so badly malformed that the chromosomes have splintered."

"Why   is   the   DNA   so   messed   up?"

"It, or she if you want to go by appearances, has 108 active Psy sites."

"But there are only..."

"She has five new ones." Tanaka cut the Prime Minister off, "If the world survives their fight, I'm guaranteed the next Nobel Prize."

"If?"

"Yes, sir. 'If.'"

Tenriki leaned against the bright red tori gate, named for the birds with a propensity for perching on the mantel of the square archway. Behind him, the car he had stolen was still idling. The damage inflicted on the car and surroundings by his mad dash probably totaled in the hundreds of thousands, but the sword in this shrine was priceless.

Nagoya was a bustling city, even this late at night. He could hear the sounds of traffic from the streets boxing in the

Atsuta Shrine on this city block, but as he staggered through the tori gate, the background grew mute, as if showing its respect for the holy site.

From here it was a long straight walk to the main shrine. Weak as his body was, Tenriki dared not spare the mental energy to carry himself the distance. It would have been a pleasant stroll of 10 minutes to reach the shine. Tenriki covered the distance five minutes; taking no notice of the minor shrines on either side, some of which were so small that prayers had to be offered while standing outside.

Tenriki stopped just inside the final tori gate. The same irrational compulsion which had forced him to remove his shoes before stepping on the tatami, now drove him to the decorated stone water basin. A white rooster roosting on the edge of the basin stared at him, trying to decide if this odd human was threatening enough to be worth giving up his perch.

Tenriki dipped one of the simple wooden ladles into the water. He splashed the water over each of his hands in turn, then took a sip and swished the water in his mouth. His throat burned, begging for the water in his mouth. Instead of swallowing he spit, spit out his symbolic impurities. He was Emperor, by definition, he could not be impure, but he still had to wash away the filth of daily life before entering a shrine. Especially a shrine housing Imperial property.

He staggered into the main building. It was little more than a covered walkway with giant purple lanterns emblazon with the Imperial Chrysanthemum and a picture window framing the large wooden doors of the inner shine, only a couple dozen meters away. Tenriki leaned heavily on the donation box blocking the way to the inner sanctum. At his will, the doors of the rear building swung open revealing an empty sword stand.

"Looking for this?"

Tenriki spun, struggling to maintain his balance.

Momo stood in the courtyard, twirling a katana with unnatural ease.

"No." Tenriki snarled, "It took centuries to develop the katana, old Japanese swords were straight blades."

"Fool. This is Ama-no-hayokiri, the Herb Quelling Dragon Sword, found by Susa-no-Wo in the tail of a dragon he slew. He gave it to his sister Amataratsu-Omikami, to apologize for some indiscretions." Momo pointed the sword at Tenriki, "No one crafted

112

it. Humans needed centuries to learn to forge blades that imitate it. Want it?"

"Yes!" Tenriki roared.

"Well," he sheathed the sword. "You can't have it." With that he sprinted away.

Tenriki ran out the back of the viewing pavilion, on an intercept course, but Momo covered the ground with remarkable speed. The woods at the edge of the clearing were dense, practically impenetrable, but Momo leapt into them and disappeared. Tenriki knew the wooded stand was only about 3 meters wide, but he also knew that by the time he had fought through that distance, the boy would have disappeared into the city.

The would-be-Emperor collapsed to his hands and knees. He was too exhausted to stand, and his mind too clouded to move his body psychically. He shivered in the cool night, his body coated in sweat, his shirt still in tatters from the battle in Ueno Park.

His ears detected the repetitious thumping about the same time he felt the approach of a familiar mind.

Angel opened the door of the Self Defense Force chopper as it touched down at Atsuta shrine. She had tucked Sakura and Bara into bed and Ume's brainwaves had moved from REM into deeper sleep, indicating that his nightmare was over. With them safe, the most important thing was finding Sakura and Momo. Her only way to find them was currently on his hands and knees in the dust.

Angel stepped out and picked up Tenriki, pulling his left arm over her shoulders and shouted into his ear, "This isn't about you. I just want the children back."

"Ise. Go to Ise. The Mirror is there."

The helicopter screamed up into the sky. The upper atmosphere was even colder than the ground had been. Tenriki curled into a ball, holding his warmth close to himself. Angel smiled in spite of herself; he was little more than a child himself. She unbuttoned her uniform, exposing the standard issue t-shirt underneath and handed the thick shirt to the humbled Emperor.

Tenriki took it and put his arms down the sleeves, even though it was too small for him to button it.

"You're tired. We won't arrive in Ise until morning. Rest."

Angel took his shoulder and guided him down until his head was resting in her lap. She stroked his hair gently, and soon his muscles relaxed into sleep.

Tenriki awoke with a jerk as the helicopter bumped down on the lot where the Ise Shrine once stood and would later be rebuilt. The current shrine, the latest in the age old cycle of rebuilding the sacred structures every twenty years, was visible out the helicopter's open door.

The outer wall hid all but the straw thatched roofs of the buildings. There was a gate in the wall, for strictly ceremonial purposes, since only priests and priestesses were allowed to enter the inner courtyard. Tenriki slammed his shoulder into the gate. Predictably, it was locked. He jumped up, catching hold of the coarse wooden top. He flailed, physically and mentally. He felt Angel's hands and mind lifting him.

"Thank you," he grunted as he rolled over the barrier.

Barely getting his feet under himself in time, Tenriki landed in a crouch, at the feet of a dozen Shinto priest. He stood up, straightened Angel's shirt as best he could and stared back.

"We have humbly awaited your Imperialcy." The old priest was bent and wrinkled with age. "I did not think one as unworthy as myself would live to see your august return."

The other clergy dropped to their knees and bowed, almost touching their noses to the ground. The elder priest bowed at the waist until his torso was horizontal. Tenriki could feel the pain in his knees, caused just by standing, so he couldn't expect him to kneel. Tenriki paused, startled by their deference, "Where is the Mirror?"

"In the main sanctum, my Lord. Shall we humbly fetch it for you?"

"No, I'll get it." He started towards the largest building, stopped and turned, "The woman who brought me is on the other side of the wall, her duty to the Imperial line is not yet ended. Give her every hospitality."

Then he ran for his last chance to be Emperor, and to save his own life.

Inside was an ornate box, about a meter square and 20 centimeters deep. He picked up the gold inlaid top and flung it across the room, revealing a mass of burlap underneath. Tenriki tore down through the layers of burlap, each older than the last. Each added to protect the mirror from non-imperial eyes. He was rewarded with a glint of light. Laughing triumphantly he pulled the large, polished-iron mirror from its cocoon. Despite its fifteen hundred years of known history and untold eons before that, the mirror reflected the dim image of a disheveled young man.

Tenriki's laugh of victory caught in his throat. The eyes staring back into his were blue. He focused out from the eyes to the ivory white face. The image was no longer a dim reflection of predawn light, it was glowing with light of its own. Blinding light.

Tenriki staggered backwards dropping the mirror. But the regalia didn't hit the ground; instead it fell into the hands of the same white haired girl. The image in the mirror lined up perfectly with the blue skirt beneath it, as if the mirror was clear glass, but the lass was the only thing to show though the dull gray metal. Kiki set down the mirror on the burlap tangle in the chest.

"I won." Tenriki said weakly.

"You lost." She turned to face him, the magatama beads around her neck clicking together, "Tell me: Why do you want to be Emperor so badly?"

"You know." Tenriki ran Dr. Genshi's ultimatum through his mind for the thousandth time.

"I know, but you don't." She walked up to him and took his left cheek in her silken hand. Before Tenriki could react, Kiki stood on tip-toe to kiss him. Her lips were warm against his. She forced his mouth open slightly and a warm sweet taste, like mochi, rice paste candy, filled his mouth. He could have easily pulled away, but had no desire to.

The warmth spread to the rest of his body. Kiku dropped back down to her heels, but the sensation stayed, leaving Tenriki felling better than he had in his entire life.

"I've fixed you. Now that 'perfect' body Dr. Genshi gave you, can synthesize all of the amino acids, just like everyone else. You no longer need do exactly what he says to earn your shots."

"The doctor's bid for power is over," Momo called from the door, sword in hand.

The freedom washed over Tenriki like a wave. He could do anything he wanted. He knew exactly what he wanted. He dropped to his knees and looked at Kiku's feet, "Please let me be Emperor, if only for a day, an hour. You can prevent me from being Emperor, so only you can make me Emperor. Make me a figurehead if it

115

suits you, but I beg you, make me Emperor."

He felt something across the back of his neck. He looked up; Kiku was lowering the magatama necklace over his head.

"I've spent much time and energy to create you. Dr. Genshi was a useful tool, but I needed to do the finishing touches myself." She looked to Momo, "Give me the sword Ama-no-hayokiri."

"Aw, can't I keep it this time?"

"Give me the scabbard too."

Momo snarled, but put the sheathed sword in her hand.

"Stand and fasten this in your belt." Kiku held out the second Regalia to Tenriki.

Tenriki did as he was told, while Kiku walked away. As he finished rebuckling his belt, she returned and handed him the mirror.

"I have given you the three Regalia. You are now Emperor. The land of the Rising Sun is yours to rule or simply reign over if you so choose, but you need to remember and do honor to the source of your power. I am here to remind you." She turned to Momo, "Little Brother, you are welcome to return with me."

"Takes you long enough to get over a grudge, but I'll accept that invitation."

A section of the eastern wall crumbled to dust and the children walked out together. As they approached the outer wall of the shrine, it shuddered and fell. The first rays of the rising sun streamed over the rubble, silhouetting the two figures. The outlines became blurred, then faded away entirely.

The Emperor fell to his knees, bowed his face to touch the ground and began praying, "All praise and glory to Amataratsu-Omikami, Goddess of the Sun, highest of all the gods, elder sister to Susa-no-Wo, Founderess of the Imperial line, through whose benevolence and wisdom..."

Fable of the Fox and the Crow, Version 2.0

The scent of blood hung thick in the air, mixing with other metallic smells. A man in an almost clean shirt and work slacks stopped and sniffed. He looked down the service tunnel and saw me in the sanguine dawn. I was wearing a black t-shirt, black jeans, and leather biker boots. I looked back at him, my cybernetic eyes completely black except for the red irises. All the color drained form the man's face.

"Morning, Raven," he stammered and walked on quickly.

I wiped the sweat from my brow with my slick hand, and went back to work "salvaging" the artificial heart which was unaware that its continued beating only fed the red stream flowing to the open gutter. Instead of the precision instruments I had once used for fine-tuning electronics, I had hatchets for breaking ribs and a ghastly selection of other tools for ripping valuable cybernetics from my victims. It wasn't civilized, but it wasn't a civilized world. It was Mars in a civil war.

I heard humming and looked up. Terror tied my stomach in knots. A cute teenager, with elf-like ears poking though her long blond hair, was squatting on the filthy alley floor, combing the hair of the severed head, like another girl her age might groom a doll or a pet.

"Vixen, what are you doing?" I asked, trying not to sound unnerved.

"He looks so handsome on his reward posters. I just want them to recognize him when we collect the bounty."

Only Vixen could care what a pimp, drug runner, and cop-killer looked like. Of course, only Vixen could outdraw someone as jumped up on Hyper as he had been. Fredricko hadn't even seen it coming. While he was worrying about Raven, the bounty killer who picks the bodies clean, the true killer – Vixen – had gunned him down.

She smiled at me, her big blue eyes sparkling, "You'd better take one of the guns that's been fired, in case someone else comes along."

She grabbed the hem of her knee-length blue pleated skirt and lifted up. The gentleman in me wanted to look away, but it was the lout in me who stared at her lithe thigh and the semiautomatic pistol strapped to it. In one fluid motion she drew the weapon and tossed it at me.

I caught it by the still warm barrel with my left hand. With my right, I drew the gun from my hip holster, which was identical to the one Vixen had thrown at me. I slid my unfired gun across the steel floor to her. She scooped it up, flicked off the safety and holstered it before letting her skirt drop back into place.

When Vixen had finished the cheesecake pose, I could concentrate again. I carefully pulled the artificial heart out with my bare hands, and put it in the backpack with the fashion-plate legs and the left arm. I had intended to gouge out his eyes, but that might ruin the good looks Vixen was trying to preserve.

"Ne ne ne. Since it's breakfast time can we get a meal at The Road?"

I don't know why she stated it as a question. She controlled the money. She also did the cooking. What she meant was, "I don't want to cook and we can afford to eat out."

"Yes we can eat at The Road, but we'll have to take the head to the morgue and take this home," I said, lifting my backpack. "Remember, Ryori-san said we're not allowed to bring body parts again."

Vixen looked down and her lips stuck out in a pout. She slipped a hand under her blouse, designed to hang at the waist of her skirt without being tucked in, and touched her stomach. After a moment she smiled up at me, "I'll go the morgue, you go home, and we'll meet down at The Road."

Before I could respond, she wrapped up the head in a cloth and went skipping away. My breath came easier, knowing I was free of her gaze, if only for a short while. Shivering in the cool Martian air, I put on my leather waistcoat. I made sure I had collected all of my tools and left the beheaded, dismembered, and gutted blob to the rats and the stray dogs.

With a 'ding,' the elevator stopped on the fifty-seventh floor of Tower #4 and I stepped out. Down the right hand hallway was a door with a small plush fox hanging on it. I fumbled for my key

118

and let myself in. The room was an old habitation module from the preatmosphere colony. The entire unit was a cramped rectangle, two meters wide and three meters deep. I dodged around the table, with a hibachi, one pot, and a small wok on top and a mini-fridge stored underneath. I took off my backpack and set it against the exterior wall, in the act, bumping the only shelf. The jar on the shelf turned to watch me. That was to be expected, as the bottle contained a dozen cybernetic eyes covered in a saline solution to keep them clean.

After I removed the last bits of flesh from them, the arm and legs would go under the bed with the other cyberlimbs. Vixen thought nothing of severing a man's head to claim the bounty on it, but my idea of salvaging cyberware from the criminals seemed to be unique on Mars. So much so that Vixen named me for it.

I sprawled out on my back in the bed, and gave my muscles a moment to relax. While not large, the bed occupied over half the room, so Vixen and I had to share it. I could almost feel her head on my chest, her body pressing down on mine. She probably insisted on this sleeping arrangement so I couldn't sneak away in the night.

Of its own accord my mind drifted back to the worst day of my life: my first day on Mars. Was it a nightmare or a flashback? Too late to wonder, I spit out a mouthful of red sand, stood up and braced myself for the hundredth iteration. My eyes focused just in time to see the fist as it connected with the bridge of my nose. I stumbled against a fragment of the hull which was still warm from reentry.

"You Earthlings ain't gonna screw us no more," the over-cybered brute bellowed.

"I don't care about your revolution," I mumbled though my bloody lips.

"We don't either, but we still get to kill you." He smiled, flexing his chromed hands.

I raised my fists in a futile act of defiance. The ringing in my ears almost drowned out the gun shots. The literal killing machine in front of me crumbled as his brains sprayed my face and chest. His leather-clad companions looked around dazed. One by one they dropped, twitching, screaming, or vomiting blood.

I stood alone, waiting. A pretty little school girl in a blue pleated skirt, white shirt, and red neckerchief sauntered into view with a smoking gun in each hand, "I like the way you stood up to them, but that spirit will get you killed... unless you have me to watch your back. I don't want anyone to know I'm a bounty hunter because they wouldn't like me. If you'll turn in the heads for me, we can share the money."

She looked at me pensively, her eyes misting, as she tightened her grip on her pistols. Was she going to kill me or kiss me? My head swam. Finally I managed, "What's your name?"

"Doesn't matter." She shook her head, tossing blonde locks around her pointed ears, "You give me a name. Then when I think of a good name, I'll give it to you."

The world was a blur, the only thing in focus was her face, cosmetically modified ears included. Only one name fit.

"Vixen!" I sat up in bed, back in the present, sweating and gasping. My body hurt in places I hadn't known I could feel pain until that day. The phantom wounds faded to memories and scars.

I got out of bed. If I was late getting down to The Road, I'd have to explain myself to that pointy eared Angel of Death.

On my way out I turned right, stepping up into the bathroom. I had to rotate the single faucet so that it was over the sink instead of the bath tub. Above the tub, which required sitting with your knees folded halfway to your chest, hung my only spare set of clothes, identical to the ones I was wearing. Vixen's change of clothes hung next to mine. It had been over half a Martian year since I moved in, but I still noticed her bra and panties drip drying every time I came into the bathroom. I washed my face and hands with the same strong soap used for our clothes.

Once in the hall, I closed the front door and relocked it. The fox bounced on her string and looked back at me. Despite our austere lifestyle, Vixen had found the money for that decoration shortly after receiving her name from me.

"The Road" wasn't the real name of the restaurant where Vixen wanted to eat. It didn't have a real name, in fact it wasn't a real restaurant. It was a large cargo crate with the top half of one side cut out to make a counter. The customers sat on fifty-gallon drums under an equally cobbled together awning.

Back on Earth, the Road would have been shut down before it ever opened. Ryori-san's limited space meant he had to prepare raw meat and finished food in the same place. Above the stove, the blackened grease was baked on the wall three centimeters thick.

Smoke drifted around the crate and awning unable to find a way out. Pity he couldn't operate on Earth, because he made the best stir-fry in the solar system.

Next to The Road was its namesake, a paved strip reaching out to the horizon in both directions. Providing food and fuel to people traveling that stretch of highway was the only legitimate source of income for the city. The blacktop ribbon was the only thing that connected us to the rest of Mars. To the East was Neo Dover, a Separatist state. To the West, New Chicago, a Loyalist stronghold.

In between the two enemies was this worthless rat-hole, called Shahiff in the middle of an even more worthless desert. Neither side wanted Shahiff, nor could they stand to let the other have it. However, it was in their common interest not to have an unchecked den of thieves on their boarder. Thus both sides offered bounties for the death of particular criminals passing through or operating in Shahiff.

Ryori-san looked up when he heard me settle onto an oil barrel, "Raven! Good thing you didn't get here any later, I was about to throw out tonight's oil. Where's your love toy?"

"She'll be along."

The overweight oriental cook leaned over to me, "I don't make it a point to listen to the customers' conversations, but there was a newcomer asking questions about you."

"Sounds normal."

"And about Vixen."

That wasn't normal. "Vixen's a big girl; she can take care of herself."

I was starting to worry about Vixen when a distant scream rung though the still morning air, "Raven!"

I leapt from under the canopy and drew my gun. Ryori-san hit the floor. No one else was around. For the first time in my life, I used the binocular enhancement in my eyes and searched the distance.

On one of the open-air walkways, midway up the central skyscrapers I saw a hulking brute with buzz-cut black hair. He held a submachine gun in each hand, raising them over his head. I checked the catwalk on either side of him, and my heart caught in my throat.

Vixen was with him, crucified. Blood dripped slowly from her outstretched wrists and her ankles. Her head was tipped forward, blond hair floating on the breeze.

My vision snapped back to normal. Ryori-san was looking at me from behind the counter.

Whoever that guy was, if he could defeat Vixen, I didn't have a chance. Why should I save the perky school girl who kept me a prisoner to terror, who forced me to endure the stigma for her killings? No one would be surprised if Raven let Vixen go and found a new 'love toy.' But I, Raven, didn't want a new lover. I wanted... I wanted to get my head examined to find out why I was about to fight, and die, to keep that little she-demon in my life.

After a quick stop by our quarters, I stepped out onto the walkway sweating and shaking. The bridges all around me were filled with spectators. They cheered at the appearance of the hometown favorite. Vixen's limp form was suspended behind my opponent, any missed shot had a chance of hitting her. He must have been smarter than he looked. He'd almost have to be if he could lace up his own army boots.

His massive hands were twitching, moving towards the Uzis slung on shoulder straps under each arm.

"You have the advantage over me!" I called out.

He stopped and looked at me. The audience went silent.

"You know who I am. But I never kill someone without knowing his name." And the crowd went wild.

"Stritous Pren."

"Well Stritous, guns are fine for killing bounty targets, but for bouts of honor like this," I unbuckled my gun belt and tossed it to the floor, "I think a more skilled weapon is required."

I reached behind my back and pull my pair of cyberware harvesting hatchets from my pocket. I tossed one to the ground in front of him.

He glared at me, then down at the hand ax. His eyes darted from side to side, looking at the assembled people. Stritous had constructed this gladiator pit, now he had to play by its rules. He dropped his firearms and knelt to pick up the scarlet hatchet.

As soon as Stritous took his eyes off me, I sprang at him. He looked up as I closed to melee range, both my hands gripping the ax in an overhead swing. His left arm came up to shield his head. The ax reverberated in my hands as it struck his radius. Something smacked my left knee. I hobbled backwards. I think he

122

had hit me with the broadside of his hatchet.

We circled each other. Every step caused a sharp pain in my knee, but at least it was still moving. Stritous' left hand was limp, coated in blood. Suddenly, he was almost on top of me. I backpedaled, bouncing off the guardrail. I counter struck, but he had moved and was swinging at my unguarded chest. I contorted my body, flinging myself off balance, but escaping his blow. Pain registered in dozens of places on and in my body. There was no way of telling which wounds he had inflicted, and which had been caused by colliding with the railing and the floor.

When the world slowed back down to my speed, I was standing in front of Vixen with Stritous lumbering towards me. If I dodged, he might hit her. I had to act first.

I lunged at his left. As predicted, he sidestepped. I spun in midair and swung at the ax coming towards my drawn out body. I struck it below the head at the thinnest part of the handle. The combined velocity of our swings embedded the edge three-quarters of the way though the wood.

I landed on my back with a thud. Stritous was over the top of me, pressing his ax down, perpendicular to the bridge of my nose. His right foot to stomped repeatedly on my sternum making it impossible for me to breathe. The blade over my face crept lower.

I twisted my hatchet. With a snap, the handle of the other broke. The head fell, cutting a gash in my forehead. My weapon continued on its arc, striking Stritous' right thigh.

He toppled forward, his bulk landing on top of me. We rolled together, and came to a stop with him on his back and me sitting on his chest, pinning his arms with my legs. Inexplicably, my hands were empty, so I punched him in the face. He struggled to get up. I punched him again. And again and again, until I had no feeling left in my hand, until my shoulder muscles burned in exhaustion, until blood was pouring from his now flattened and misaligned nose. Eventually his consciousness got tired of being hit. Stritous' muscles went lax and his eyes started to roll aimlessly in their sockets.

I left him and rushed to Vixen. I lifted her head under the chin, she was now eye level with me. All the color was gone from her face, her eyes were closed.

Fumbling in my waistcoat pockets, I found I still had my 'surgery' pliers. I put my left arm around Vixen's waist and lifted her. She inhaled sharply with me supporting her weight, and began to breathe normally again. I slid the pliers between her left wrist and the sheet of construction plastic behind her. In a moment, the industrial nail binding the two gave way. I freed the right wrist and then her ankles. I knew enough to leave the spikes in Vixen to inhibit the bleeding until I could get her to a body shop.

I turned, Vixen cradled in my arms, her head against my left shoulder. Stritous was standing up, leaning to keep weight off his wounded right leg, holding one of his sub-machineguns.

"Did you think you were Mimi's first partner?" he spat with a spray of blood.

Vixen's unconscious form shifted in my arms. The pistol strapped to her left leg brushed my fingers: the fully loaded pistol she had taken from me this morning.

"I know your secret, but now I've proven her wrong! I caught her off guard and unarmed, proving I'm better. Now I'm going to prove I'm better than you!"

I couldn't think of a snappy comeback, so just I drew the gun and fired through Vixen's skirt. Stritous' jaw dropped. His puffy eyes went wide, almost getting back to normal size.

I walked forward to improve my aim, and fired again and again and again. He dropped to his knees, then collapsed entirely. I stood over him and loosed the final three round burst into his face. If he had a price on his head, I had just ruined the brain for collecting the bounty. But all that mattered was making sure he wouldn't hurt Vixen again.

The audience dispersed and I took Vixen to the nearest back alley doctor.

Vixen woke up that afternoon in her own bed. She opened her eyes and let out a whimper. An instant later she bolted upright and looked around frantically. Her eyes fixed on me, sitting in our only chair at her bedside, and she threw her arms around my neck.

"Raven!"

Then she noticed the bandages encircling her wrists and hands like fingerless gloves. She recoiled, eyes wide and misting, her mouth agape.

"It's okay. You lost a lot of blood. Your wrists and ankles were badly damaged, but with time and work you'll get full use back. You're going to be all right."

She looked down at her hands, now lying haphazard in her

lap, "Why didn't you have them replaced?"

"Bones didn't have anything as pretty as your natural hands."

Vixen paused uncomfortably, "And the man?"

"Stritous is dead, Mimi."

"Who?" Vixen shook her head as if clearing it. The motion caused a tassel of blonde strands to cascade down her forehead and across her face, "Oh, yes. The girl I used to be. Mimi no longer means anything. I am Vixen."

She tried to brush the hair out of her face with her wrists. After the third unsuccessful swipe, I gingerly pinched the hairs and tucked them behind one of her pointed ears.

"Thank you," she said downcast.

"Right," I cleared my throat, "We'll need to get you a nurse for while you're healing. You'll need help eating, dressing, bathing. I'd be lying if I said I wouldn't enjoy the job but..."

"I want you to enjoy it."

"What?"

"I said please enjoy my body." Vixen was looking away, her cheeks turning bright red, "I didn't say anything when you were scared of me, because you'd do whatever I told you and it wouldn't mean anything. But now that I'm defenseless, no, I mean I'd like it if... if you want to..."

I touched Vixen's cheek, "I promise. But first you need to eat something and try to start healing."

I was boiling water when there was a knock on the door. It was probably just someone interested in buying salvaged cybernetics, but after this morning's episode, I wasn't willing to chance anything. I had forgotten my own gun back at the bridge. Vixen's thigh holsters were sitting on the shelf next to the eyes. I had cleaned and reloaded both pistols to pass the time. I grabbed one and moved to the door.

I flung open the door. The gun was pointed at the ceiling, but I was ready to level it. Ryori-san jumped when he saw me. I let out a breath I didn't realize I had been holding and addressed our visitor, "Yes?"

"Raven, the Neo Dover Army is coming to occupy Shahiff. You have to get out of town."

"Thanks for you're concern, but I'm not a Loyalist. They won't kill me just because I'm from Earth. Sorry, Separatists call it Terra."

"It's more than that. The guy you offed today in front of everyone was one of their advance scouts."

"How do you know that?" I knew the answer as soon as I finished the question. I aimed point blank at Ryori-san's face, "You're a spy, you filthy lying…"

He put up his hands and backed away, "Only as a sideline."

"There was nothing political about it!" I yelled as I walked after him, maintaining my aim, "He was a demented sadist who tortured a school girl to pick a fight with me, so I gave him his fight!"

"I know. I know. That's why I told them you stopped by my place to say good-bye before leaving town."

I glared at him.

"If they find you, it's going to be bad, and if they find you here, it's going to be bad for me too."

"I'll be gone by sundown," I spat. Turning I saw Vixen framed in our doorway, watching me downcast, "Make that sun-up. I have a promise to keep before leaving."

As the sun rose over the scarlet horizon, I lowered my head to step inside the canopy attached to the packing crate/restaurant sitting next to the highway. It was a difficult maneuver. My backpack was heavy with supplies, which had cost nearly everything we had, Vixen was in my arms, the stuffed fox from our door peeking out of her breast pocket.

"Raven!" Ryori-san's eyes went wide.

"I didn't want to make a liar out of you, so I came to say goodbye."

"Right. Goodbye," he said stiffly.

"Sayonara Ryori-san!" Vixen chirped enthusiastically, with a Japanese accent.

"Sayonara Vixen-chan," Ryori-san replied.

Leaving The Road, I carried Vixen towards the assorted vehicles parked along the roadside. In a convoy of six heavily laden cargo trucks, I approached a man dressed in black, standing at the head of the line.

"Excuse me."

The man who turned around had white hairs sprinkled in among his short brown hairs. His face had started to sag with age. His entire outfit was black, except for the white preacher collar.

126

"Do you have room for two hitchhikers?"

He looked at Vixen's hands, "What great evil has been visited upon you, my child?" He looked back to me, "The Lord's Hospital has never turned away those in need of mercy. We will treat your sister, but we won't be leaving until we can start all of our trucks."

Looking down the line, I could see that the forth from the front had its hood up. I walked to it, knelt down and set Vixen against the large tire.

Five minutes later I had traced the problem to a faulty sensor in the motor. I couldn't fix it without parts, but by unplugging two of the fail-safes, I could make the truck's computer forget about it. I gave a thumbs up to the simply dressed woman behind the wheel and moved to the side. The electric motor hummed to life as I picked up Vixen.

The woman jumped out of the cab, rosary beads bouncing around her neck. She bent over and looked Vixen in the face, "Your brother's quite the mechanic. Could you talk him into joining our cause?"

Vixen looked up at me ingenuously, "Will you help them, big brother?"

"Yes."

Two other people helped me climb into the back of one of the cargo transports with Vixen. I settled between a couple of crates with Vixen on my lap.

"After the church ostracized me as an "Android-Lover" back on Terra, I never thought I'd end up a missionary mechanic."

"After I heal, I'll be a nurse!"

"Do you know anything about medicine?"

"I know a lot about injuries."

I smiled, "I guess at some point we'll have to tell them we're not siblings."

"Why?"

"Because I want to make love to you again," I said in exasperation.

She looked at me, eyes glistening, "They say our love is wrong, but I don't believe them. I love you, big brother, and I know it's right."

I let out a sigh. For the past four hundred or so days I had played the role of a bounty killer. A reputation for incest couldn't be much worse. But in the end I had lived up to my tough reputation and killed Stritous. Who was I to say where the line between fiction and reality was drawn? Maybe this pretty little girl pressed against my chest really was my sister.

"Sister, dear, what's your name?"

"Mary. What's yours, big brother?"

"John."

About the Author

Ramsey "Tome Wyrm" Lundock uses his nickname instead of his "meat body" name in e-mail. His first article "Marybelle for Arrivers" appeared in *Polyhedron* in 1999, published by the gone but not forgotten TSR. In college he was involved in the RPGA, eventually rising to the position of Living Verge Campaign Director.

He graduated from the University of Florida in 2002, with degrees in physics and Japanese, and went to work on the family longhorn cattle and thoroughbred horse farm. On June 7th, 2003, he had the incomparable thrill of watching their horse Supervisor run in the Belmont Stakes, finishing fifth. Ramsey continued to work on the farm and write freelance until restlessness drove him back to academia in 2005.

He enrolled in the Tohoku University graduate Astronomy Graduate program. His first scientific paper as primary author appeared in *Astronomy & Astrophysics* in 2009. In 2009, Ramsey published two articles in the English edition of the Asahi Newspaper (which is also the Japanese edition of the New York Times.) One article about Japanese castles and the second about his trip to a real life Devils' Island. In 2010, he wrote an article about his travel and research for the Tohoku University sciences magazine. At the same time, he was lead designer for the *Infinite Futures RPG* which was released by Avalon Game Company in 2011. Although he has had stories in numerous anthologies, *Bleeding Edge* is his first solo book.

SEASONS OF DEATH
THE SMOKY MOUNTAINS MURDERS
by Marlene Mitchell, Gary Yeagle

In the fall of 1969 in the mountains of eastern Tennessee, a poor backwoods farmer and his wife were brutally shot and killed by four drunken hunters, along with their three dogs, horse and two fawns. The farmer's two young sons managed to escape but were unable to identify the killers. Now decades later, someone has decided to take revenge.
[Murder Mystery, ages 14+]

CIRCLE OF PREY
by Marlene Mitchell

Ambition. Wealth. Greed. Power.
Truths turning to lies, father against son, friends becoming enemies, predator turning into prey and the circle continues.
Pitting man against the largest and one of the smartest animals on the planet makes for an interesting turn of events as you follow the journey of Jakuta, a bull elephant who is the ultimate prey.
[Modern Thriller, ages 14+]

TRAJAN'S ARCH

by Michael Williams

Gabriel Rackett has written one novel and has no prospects of writing another, his powers stagnated by drink and loss. Into his possession comes a childhood friend's manuscript, taking him back to the ghosts that haunted his own coming-of-age. Gabriel returns to his old haunts through a series of fantastic stories that preoccupy and pursue him back to their dark secret sources.
[Literate Fantasy Realism, ages 18+]

AN UNFORGIVING LAND

by Jason Walters

This collection of horrific short stories from Nevada's Black Rock Desert will give you nightmares for years to come. The very landscape of the desert it portrays seems to have a will of its own, as if possessed by a violent, hideous determination to purge all visitors from its bosom. It suffers only those few individualistic, rugged souls who need nothing from the outside world to dwell within its confines.
[Horror Short Stories, ages 18+]